MARVEL CINEMATIC UNIVERSE

PHASE THREE

MARVEL

DOCTOR
STRANGE

UNIVERSE
E E

STRANGE

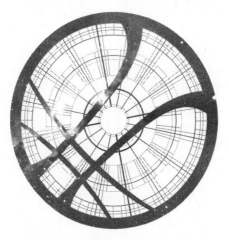

Adapted by Alex Irvine

Based on a screenplay by
Jon Spaihts and Scott Derrickson, & C. Robert Cargill

Produced by Kevin Feige

Directed by Scott Derrickson

L B

LITTLE, BROWN AND COMPANY
New York   Boston

© 2017 MARVEL.

Excerpt from *Phase One: Marvel's Thor* copyright © 2015 MARVEL

Cover illustration by Danny Haas

Little, Brown and Company
Hachette Book Group
1290 Avenue of the Americas, New York, NY 10104
Visit us at lb-kids.com
marvelkids.com

First Edition: June 2017

Little, Brown and Company is a division of Hachette Book Group, Inc.
The Little, Brown name and logo are trademarks of Hachette Book Group, Inc.

The publisher is not responsible for websites (or their content) that are not owned by the publisher.

Library of Congress Control Number 2017933407

ISBNs: 978-0-316-27159-2 (hardcover); 978-0-316-31415-2 (ebook)

Printed in the United States of America

LSC-C

10 9 8 7 6 5 4 3 2 1

PROLOGUE

The sorcerer Kaecilius and a select group of his Zealots entered the dark interior of the library of Kamar-Taj through a portal he had created. He had not been in that room since leaving the magical order years before...and he never expected to return again. After tonight, he would have no need of it. There was no greater collection of magical knowledge in the world. Kaecilius had read many of the books before. He was, at last, ready to read one that had been long denied him.

The librarian and other sorcerers present saw the group enter with purpose, and immediately recognized Kaecilius. They started to cast spells for their defense, but he was too quick—and far too powerful. His acolytes had Space Shards, blades created by magical force that could cut any physical substance. Kaecilius wielded those, as well as crackling whips of energy unfurled from the sling rings all the sorcerers of Kamar-Taj wore. He bound their leader, tying his wrists and holding him while his Zealots disposed of the others. It was all over quickly. The acolytes fought bravely, but were doomed by Kaecilius's superior power.

Then he walked across the chamber, passing a projection of planet Earth turning slowly, the lights of its cities sparkling in the near darkness.

Kaecilius strode confidently to The Ancient One's own shelf, where *The Book of Cagliostro*, one of the mightiest texts of Earth's mystical orders, waited for him. It contained magical spells and rituals collected over thousands of years. Kaecilius knew some of them already and had no interest in some of the others—but one ritual in the book had obsessed him since he had first learned of it early in his study with The Ancient One. One of Kaecilius's strengths was his careful patience—he knew well the dangers of attempting the ritual too soon . . . but now he was ready. He paged through the book and found the ritual. Its words rang in his mind and he could feel the power within them, even though he dared not speak them here. For a moment he contemplated taking the entire book, but he liked the idea of leaving it incomplete. Everyone who ever touched it after this moment would see the mark he had left. Kaecilius tore out the pages he needed and dropped the book on the floor.

"Master Kaecilius." He knew that voice. "That ritual will bring you only sorrow."

He turned to see a slight figure entering the sanctum. She wore a yellow hooded robe that hid her face, but he did not have to see her to know her presence. Kaecilius gestured and a portal opened. He and his Zealots ran through it and out onto a London street. They strode along the sidewalk, doubting that their pursuer would provoke a battle in the center of the city.

They were wrong. In front of them a barrier appeared, like a shattered mirror reflecting a thousand images of themselves. The Mirror Dimension. They could not pass the barrier, nor leave this place without fighting their way free of her. When they turned, Kaecilius saw the figure walking calmly toward them.

"Hypocrite!" he screamed. She wanted all power for herself. She wanted to keep her students ignorant and make them her servants—but Kaecilius was done serving. Now he was ready to be the master.

He and the Zealots brought forth their energy whips, but the hooded figure raised her arms and made a sweeping gesture. The entire street, and the buildings on either side, tilted over until the facades of the buildings were below Kaecilius's feet. The sinister group fell and regained their balance, scrambling to face her, but she was not done yet. With another gesture she turned the window frames and cornices on the buildings into churning gears. Some of the Zealots were caught and swept into them. Kaecilius dodged the gears, staying on solid ground. The rest of the Zealots attacked. They thought by getting close to her they could overcome her superior magical powers, but they underestimated her. With a twitch of her fingers she made a magical fan appear in one hand, a half circle made of arcane energy. She deflected their attacks and threw the fan, striking down the Zealots before they could surround her. Even those who got close found that she was more than they could handle. She fought with both mystic power and martial arts. The Zealots could barely touch her.

Kaecilius himself had no desire to fight her at that moment. He had the pages from the book. She gestured again and wrenched the entire streetscape another ninety degrees over. Now Kaecilius and the Zealots were hanging on to the upside-down building that a moment ago had been the ground beneath their feet.

He pointed down and opened a portal. The Zealots' attack had bought him enough time. When the portal was open, the few remaining Zealots jumped and dropped off the building, falling into it before the churning windows could grind them away. Kaecilius clutched the pages of the book and jumped himself, diving headfirst through the portal and out of the Mirror Dimension.

It flickered and disappeared as soon as he had passed.

The warrior watched for a moment, holding her spell in case Kaecilius planned a surprise return. When that did not happen, she released the spell. The buildings and street groaned and rotated back to their natural positions as she phased herself from the Mirror Dimension back into the everyday world. She stepped off the facade and onto the sidewalk as the windows locked themselves back into place. In moments everything was normal again. People, cars, and bicycles once again flooded the street. As she walked away, she flipped her hood back. Her shaven head and yellow robe attracted a few glances, but this was London. No one looked at her for too long.

Kaecilius had made his move. The Ancient One had expected it for a long time, and now that it had happened, she had to make sure he never had a chance to use those pages.

CHAPTER 1

Doctor Stephen Strange was having a typical day, tapping his foot to a funk soundtrack as he performed a delicate repair on a patient with a highly unusual heart problem. Every surgery he did took place in the hospital's main operating theater so medical students could watch him work. He was the best in the world at what he did. He knew everything there was to know about the human body, and he had the rock-steady hands and the nerve to try surgeries that ordinary doctors thought were impossible.

He also liked to play musical trivia while he worked.

One of his head nurse Billy's jobs was to keep a playlist going and challenge Strange's musical knowledge. Strange was never wrong. Never.

"Challenge round, Billy," he said. Usually, Billy played him a mix of old rock and funk music. During the challenge rounds he was allowed to go to other kinds of music.

Billy tapped the SKIP button on the operating-room console. Smooth jazz filled the air. "Oh, come on, Billy," Strange said. "You've got to be messing with me."

"No, Doctor." Billy sounded so smug that Strange took a little extra pleasure in hitting him with an immediate answer.

"1977," he declared after rattling off the name of

an obscure album. "Honestly, Billy, you said this one would be hard."

"Ha!" Billy said. "It's 1978."

"No, Billy, while the song may have *charted* in 1978, the album was released in December 1977."

"No, no. Wikipedia says the—"

"Check again." This, Strange thought, was the difference between him and ordinary people. They knew a little and thought they knew a lot. He knew a lot, period.

"Where do you store all this useless information?" asked his surgical partner, Doctor Bruner.

"Useless? The man charted a top ten hit with a flugelhorn." Strange was certain that had only happened once. "Status, Billy?" he prompted.

Billy sighed. "1977."

"Oh please. I hate you," Doctor Bruner grumbled.

"Whoa! Feels so good, doesn't it?" Strange chuckled at his own joke, then glanced up as he saw someone at the door. It was Doctor Christine Palmer, Strange's colleague—and his ex-girlfriend.

"Oh," Bruner said when she saw Christine. "I've got this, Stephen. You've done your bit. Go ahead, we'll close up."

Out in the hall, Christine handed him a tablet with images of a patient's very badly damaged brain. "What is that?" he asked.

"GSW," she said, using the doctors' shorthand for a gunshot wound.

He swiped through the images. "It's amazing you kept him alive. Apneic, further brain stem testing after reflex test…I think I found the problem, Doctor Palmer. You left a bullet in his head."

"Thanks," she said dryly. "It's impinging on the medulla. I needed a specialist. Nic diagnosed brain death. Something about that doesn't feel right to me."

Strange looked more closely at the image. Something about the bullet…Ah. He knew what had happened, and knew they would have to act fast to stop Nic West from doing something stupid. "We have to run."

They caught up to Nic West wheeling the patient into another operating room. "Doctor West!" Christine called. "What are you doing? Hey!"

"Organ harvesting," West answered. "He's a donor."

"Slow down. I did not agree to that."

"I don't need you to," he said, starting to get irritated. "We've already called brain death."

"Prematurely," Strange cut in. "We need to get him prepped for a suboccipital craniotomy."

West shook his head. "I'm not going to let you operate on a dead man."

Strange held up the image that had caught his attention. "What do you see?"

"A bullet?"

"A perfect bullet." Most bullets were squashed out of shape when they punched into a human body. This one wasn't. That was the clue that Strange had latched on to. "It's been hardened," he explained. "You harden a bullet by alloying lead with antimony. A toxic metal. And as it leaks directly into the cerebral spinal fluid..."

West understood. "Rapid onset central nervous system shutdown."

Christine turned the gurney around. "We need to go."

"The patient's not dead, but he's dying. Do you still want to harvest his organs?" Strange couldn't resist the little jab at Doctor West.

"I'll assist you," West offered.

"No, Doctor Palmer will assist me. Thank you." They left West there and got to the operating room as fast as they could. There wasn't much time. Strange used a tiny blade to open the smallest possible path to the bullet. When he was done, he handed it to Christine.

"Thank you," she said quietly.

Now they had to retract the bullet. The patient's brain was still bleeding. "Image guidance, stat," she called.

Normally, a surgeon would use a tiny robotic arm to extract a bullet from such a delicate part of the body, but Strange knew they didn't have the minutes they would have to wait. "We do not have time for that."

"You can't do it by hand," Christine objected.

"I can and I will."

"This isn't the time for showing off, Strange," Doctor West said. He had caught up and was observing from the far end of the operating room.

"How about ten minutes ago, when you called the wrong time of death?" Strange shot back. He never took his eyes off what he was doing. "Cranial nerves intact," he noted. If—when—he got the bullet out, the patient would recover.

A nurse rolled the image guidance screen up to the operating table, even though Strange wasn't using it. On it everyone could see the surgical pliers reaching slowly toward the bullet.

Strange noticed a tiny flash of reflected light out of the corner of his eye. He couldn't afford the slightest distraction. "Doctor West, cover your watch."

West did. Everyone in the operating room held their breaths as Strange pushed the pliers deeper into the patient's brain, avoiding the most critical nerves and blood vessels. His hands were steady and perfect, as always. He found the bullet, feeling the touch of it through the pliers in his fingertips. Slowly and evenly, he drew it out. It gleamed in the surgical lamps, and he dropped it into a pan.

After that, closing the patient up was child's play. He left that to Doctor West. Then he delivered the good news to the patient's family, and even accepted a hug. "You know," Christine said as they walked toward the break room, "you didn't have to humiliate him in front of everyone."

"I didn't have to save his patient, either," Strange pointed out. "But, you know, sometimes I just can't help myself."

"Nic is a great doctor."

Not as great as I am, Strange thought with more than a little characteristic bemusement. "You came to me."

"Yeah, well, I needed a second opinion."

"You had a second opinion. What you needed was a competent one."

"Well, all the more reason why you should be my neurosurgeon on call." Christine was the head surgeon in the emergency room. "You could make such a difference."

"I can't work in your butcher shop," Strange said. Over her objection, he went on. "Look, I'm using trans-sectioned spinal cords to stimulate neurogenesis in the central nervous system. My work is at least going to save thousands for years to come. In the ER, I get to save one drunk idiot with a gun."

"Yeah, you're right. In the ER, you're only saving lives. There's no fame, there's no interviews... Well, I guess I'll have to stick with Nic."

"Oh, wait a minute. You're not...you guys aren't..."

"What?"

"Sorry, I thought that was implicit in my disgust."

"Explicit, actually. And no, I have a very strict rule against dating colleagues."

"Oh, really?" He was living proof that she hadn't always had that rule.

"I call it the Strange Policy." She had set him up.

Ouch, Strange thought. But he didn't let her know she had gotten to him. "Oh, good! I'm glad something is named after me. You know, I invented a laminectomy procedure, and yet, somehow, no one seems to want to call it the Strange technique."

"*We* invented that technique," she corrected him.

"Well, regardless, I'm very flattered by your policy." He missed her. It was hard to admit, but it was true. "Look," he said. "I'm talking tonight at a Neurological Society dinner. Come with me."

"Another speaking engagement?" Christine rolled her eyes. "So romantic."

"You used to love going to those things with me. We had fun together."

"No." She laughed. "*You* had fun. They weren't about us; they were about you."

"Not only about me."

"Stephen," she said, and now she was still smiling but sad at the same time. "Everything is about you." She started to walk away.

"Maybe we can hyphenate," he called after her. "Strange-Palmer technique."

"Palmer-Strange," she called back. Then she was gone.

He took his time getting ready for the Neurological Society dinner, and when he left his loft—a full floor in Lower Manhattan—Strange knew he was looking good. He gunned his car out into the evening traffic, loving the way it felt. He was almost as good a driver as he was a surgeon, and he drove as if he were on a racetrack. He was outside the city on a winding two-lane road when Billy called in. He always had Billy on the lookout for interesting cases.

"Billy! What have you got for me?"

"I've got a thirty-five-year-old Air Force colonel. Crushed his lower spine in some kind of experimental armor. Mid-thoracic vertebral fracture."

"Well, I could help, but so can fifty other people.

Find me something worth my time." Strange didn't waste his talent on patients any *ordinary* neurosurgeon could fix.

"I have a sixty-eight-year-old female with an advanced brain stem glioma."

That was a death sentence no matter who the surgeon was. "Yeah, you want me to screw up my perfect record? Definitely not."

"How about a twenty-two-year-old female with an electronic implant in her brain to control schizophrenia struck by lightning?"

"That does sound interesting. Could you send me the..." His phone pinged and images appeared. "Got it." He glanced from the road down to the image, then back to the road. He swung into the other lane to pass the car in front of him. Then he looked back down to the image.

Then he made a mistake.

His car scraped the other car's fender and careened away. Strange hauled at the wheel, but it was too late. He spun off the road and crashed into a tree. Then he kept going down a steep bluff, smashing through other trees and plowing into the ground on the bank of the Hudson River. The last thing he saw before he passed out was blood on his hands.

Then ... nothing.

CHAPTER 2

When Strange woke up, he was in a hospital bed. Christine was by his side. "Hey," she said softly. "It's okay. It's going to be okay." He had no idea what day it was, or how long he had been out.

His eyes started to focus. The left was swollen mostly shut. He looked at her, then down the bed. For a long moment all he could do was stare. Both of his hands were in traction, with a frame of pins and brackets screwed into them. Fixators, they were called. Doctors only used them in cases of catastrophic damage. Strange tried to move his fingers and couldn't. All he could do was twitch his thumbs a little. "What did they do?" he croaked slowly and painfully. Already he was thinking like a surgeon, thinking about what he would have done.

"They rushed you in a chopper. But it took a little while to find you. Golden hours for nerve damage went by while you were in the car."

"What did they do?" he asked again. He didn't care about the golden hours or the helicopter. He cared about his hands. Without them...he wasn't sure what he was. He was nothing.

"Stainless steel pins in the bones," she said. "There were multiple torn ligaments. Severe nerve damage in both hands. You were on the table for eleven hours."

"Look at these fixators," Strange moaned.

"No one could have done better," Christine said.

He knew she meant it, but he turned his head to look at her and said, "I could have done better."

It was an agonizing two weeks before they removed the fixators and let him try moving his hands on his own. He held them up, crooked and scarred and shaking. "No," he said. He couldn't believe this was happening. "No."

"Give your body time to heal," Doctor Patel said.

He looked at her and thought, *No, this* won't *heal.* "You ruined me," he said.

He found himself in the uncomfortable position of being a patient. He had consulted with every doctor working in experimental neurosurgery, and of course had his own ideas, too. If he could increase blood flow to the hands, maybe...

"Doctor Strange," the consulting physician objected, "those tissues are still healing."

"So speed it up. Pass the stent down the brachial artery under the radial artery." He'd read about this. Even if he couldn't perform surgery, he could keep up on the medical journals.

"It's possible," another of the consulting team said. "Experimental and expensive, but possible."

That was fine with Strange. "All I need is possible," he said.

After the second operation came grueling hours of physical therapy. He had to recover strength in his hands before he had any hope of being steady enough to perform surgery again. The therapist put rubber bands around his fingertips and had him flex his fingers straight. "Up, up," he encouraged. "Show me your strength."

"*Ahhh!*" It hurt too much. "It's useless."

"It's not useless, man, you can do this." The therapist was always an optimist, and Strange was sure that was helpful to some patients. Today it made Strange furious.

"Then answer me this, Bachelor's Degree," he snapped. His hands wouldn't stop shaking. "Have you ever known anyone with nerve damage this severe to do this, and actually recover?"

"One guy, yeah," the therapist said without missing a beat. "Factory accident, broke his back. Paralyzed. His legs wasted away. He had pain in his shoulder from the wheelchair. He came in three times a week. But one day he stopped coming. I thought he was dead. A few years later, he walked past me on the street."

"*Walked?*"

"Yeah, he walked."

Strange knew better. That was impossible. "Show me his file."

"It can take me a while to pull the files from the archive," the therapist said. Then his good nature slipped a little. Strange had pushed him too far. "But if it proves you wrong, it's worth it."

Strange threw himself into the work of getting his hands back. He read everything there was to read, no matter how experimental or how dangerous. He worked constantly at getting his coordination back. But at the end of a month, he still couldn't shave his own face. He could barely write his name. His last hope was a European doctor named Doctor Etienne, who specialized in cutting-edge reconstruction. But Etienne wasn't the answer. "I looked at all your research," he said on a video call. "I read all the papers you've sent, but...none will work. I...I don't think you realize how severe the damage is. At best, I'd try and fail."

"Look, I understand. Here's the thing—" Strange began. He didn't care if it failed. He wouldn't be any worse off than he already was.

"What you want from me is impossible, Stephen. I've got my own reputation to consider," the doctor on the other end of the call interrupted.

"Etienne, wait," Strange said. But he knew what it was like to refuse a case because he didn't want to endanger his own reputation. Now he was on the other end.

"I can't help you," Etienne said, and hung up.

For a moment, Strange sat quietly. Then, in a rage, he flung everything off his desk.

There had to be something, someone...someone had to know how to repair his hands. Without them he wasn't Stephen Strange.

Christine walked into Strange's loft with a care package, only to find him sitting there dejectedly. "He won't do it," she guessed.

"He's a hack," Strange said, already on to the next idea. "There's a new procedure in Tokyo. They culture donor stem cells and then harvest them and 3-D-print a scaffold. If I could get a loan together, just a small loan, two hundred thousand—"

She cut him off. "Stephen. You've always spent money as fast as you could make it, but now you're spending money you don't even have. Maybe...it's time to consider stopping."

"No." That was unthinkable. "Now is exactly the time not to stop. Because, you see, I'm not getting any better!"

"But this isn't medicine anymore. This is mania. Some things just can't be fixed."

Strange knew this was true for other people. Not for him. If he wasn't a surgeon—a great surgeon, the greatest—what was he? "Life without my work..."

"Is still life," she said. "This isn't the end. There are other things that can give your life meaning."

He was not in the mood for her to get sentimental. "Like what? Like you?" he snapped.

That hurt her. She took a moment to compose herself and said, "This is the part where you apologize."

Not a chance, he thought. "This is the part where you leave."

"Fine," she said. "I can't watch you do this to yourself anymore."

"Too difficult for you, is it?" She didn't have the strength he had. He was going to see this through and find a solution, no matter what.

"Yes," Christine said. "It is. And it breaks my heart to see you this way."

"No. Don't pity me." That was the last thing he wanted or needed.

"I'm not pitying you," she said. But he didn't believe it.

"Oh yeah?" he shot back. "Then what are you doing here? Bringing cheese and wine as if we're old friends going for a picnic? We are not friends, Christine. You just love a sob story, don't you? Is that what I am to you now? Poor Stephen Strange, charity case. He finally needs me. Another dreg of humanity for you to work on. Fix him up and send him back into the world, heart is just humming..." He knew he was out of line but he didn't care. He wasn't going to be just a patient to her, or just someone who needed help. He was Stephen Strange. He didn't need anyone's help. "You care so much!" he shouted, bitter and sarcastic. "Don't you?"

Christine had let him rant, and now that he had run out of steam, she might have gone on a rant of her own. But all she said was, "Good-bye, Stephen." She dropped her keys on the table as she walked out.

CHAPTER 3

Later that night Strange opened a package the overly optimistic physical therapist had sent him. He didn't believe there would be anything useful in it. The guy was probably just telling him stories to motivate him. When he pulled the folder out of the envelope, the first thing he saw was a sticky note: *Told you so!*

He started reading the file. Then he read it

again. Then he realized that if he were the kind of person who apologized, he would owe the therapist an apology. Instead, he went looking for the patient from the file. It wasn't easy to find him—Strange wasn't a detective by any means, and one person in a city of millions could be hard to find.

Finally, Stephen found the patient playing basketball at a public court near the river. He was running, jumping, even talking trash to the other players. "Come on, man! Where is the competition?" He laughed.

Stephen called out to him from the other side of the fence surrounding the court. "Jonathan Pangborn," he said. The tall man with dark hair and a short but unkempt beard turned to look at him, puzzled to hear a stranger calling his name. "C7–C8 spinal cord injury, complete," Strange added.

"Who are you?" Pangborn asked.

Strange kept talking, mostly because he couldn't believe this was the same person he'd read about.

"Paralyzed from the mid-chest down. Partial paralysis of both hands."

"I don't know you," Pangborn said.

"I'm Stephen Strange. I'm a neurosurgeon. Was a neurosurgeon," he corrected himself.

"Actually, you know what, man?" Pangborn came close to the fence. "I think I know you. I came to your office once. You refused to see me. I never got past your assistant."

"You were untreatable."

Pangborn smirked. "No glory for you in that, right?"

"You came back from a place there is no way back from! I ... I'm trying to find my own way back." He held up his hands so Pangborn could see them and understand.

Pangborn paused, considering. "Hey, Pangborn, you in or out?" one of the other players called. He waved for the next game to go on and walked around the fence to meet Strange.

"All right," he said. "I'd given up on my body. I thought my mind was the only thing I had left. I should at least try to elevate that. So I sat with gurus and sacred women. Strangers carried me to mountaintops to see holy men. And finally, I found my teacher." He spoke with the quiet intensity of a man who has been through something remarkable—something he thinks no one will believe, and doesn't care if they do. "And my mind was elevated. And my spirit deepened. And somehow..."

"Your body healed," Strange finished. It was an incredible story, unbelievable. Nothing in medicine or science said it was possible. And yet there was Jonathan Pangborn, walking.

"Yes," Pangborn said. "And there were deeper secrets to learn then, but I did not have the strength to receive them. I chose to settle for my miracle, and I came back home." He looked away over the river, then quietly made a decision. "The place you're looking for is called Kamar-Taj. But the cost is high."

"How much?" Strange didn't care. He would sell everything he had to make it happen.

"I'm not talking about money," Pangborn said. He gave Strange a mocking smile. "Good luck." Then he walked away to rejoin the game.

A week later, Strange was in Nepal. He'd found mentions of Kamar-Taj in different books on mysticism, the kind of thing he would never have read before. But he'd seen Jonathan Pangborn walk and run and jump, and if the books said Kamar-Taj was in Kathmandu, Strange decided he was going to Kathmandu. He would find Kamar-Taj no matter what.

So he walked the teeming streets of Kathmandu, disheveled and bearded, his hair matted to his head and wilder than ever before, occasionally stopping someone to ask about Kamar-Taj. Most of them just shook their heads. Sometimes he would get vague directions. He did this for days. Walking through one of the temple complexes, he was pointed down a small side street. Tired and footsore, Strange kept going. He would knock on every door in Kathmandu if that's what it took.

The side street was deserted, and as soon as Strange was halfway down it, he noticed someone following him. Then a man stepped out of a doorway in front of him. "Okay," he said. He knew what was happening.

He turned so he could see all the men. There were four of them. "Guys, I don't have any money."

"Your watch," one of them said. At least they spoke English, Strange thought. Maybe he could talk his way out of this.

"No, please. It's all I have left."

The mugger didn't care. "Your watch," he repeated.

"All right." Strange reached for his wrist like he was going to take his watch off. Then something snapped inside him. No. He wasn't going to give them his watch. He wasn't going to be robbed in an alley like some stupid tourist. As the mugger reached for the watch, Strange wound up and punched him in the face.

His attack didn't do much, and the pain from his hand was incredible. For a moment it blocked out everything else. Then one of the other muggers knocked him down and all four started kicking and beating him. He tried to stand but he couldn't. One of them kicked him in the head and he curled up, trying to avoid being badly hurt. He took their abuse for what seemed like an eternity, and they only stopped when he wasn't moving anymore.

He felt one of them jerk the watch from his wrist.

Then, out of nowhere, another man appeared. He charged into the group of muggers, green-and-black hooded cloak flying out behind him as he took on all four of them. Like something out of a movie, he dodged all their attacks and beat them to the ground in the time it took Strange to regain his senses. When all four of the muggers were incapacitated, the stranger bent down and picked something up from the street. He walked to Strange, who was just getting to his feet. He was battered, but he didn't think anything was broken.

The stranger held out his watch. The face was shattered. Strange took it and nodded to thank him. He pulled back his hood. He was a young man, with short hair and a long scar that stood out on his dark forehead. When he spoke, he had an accent Strange didn't recognize. "You're looking for Kamar-Taj?"

All Strange could do was nod. Had this guy been following him? Had he heard Strange asking someone else about Kamar-Taj?

The stranger nodded back and started walking.

Strange followed, cradling his right arm. Now that he'd had a chance to settle down a little and let the adrenaline wear off, he was feeling the pain more acutely.

Winding through the streets of Kathmandu, the stranger passed a temple and led Strange into a cramped square. He nodded toward a simple wooden door set into a brick wall. "Really? Are you sure you got the right place?" Strange asked. Looking back at the temple, he added, "That one looks a little more...Kamar-Taj-y."

Deadly serious, Strange's rescuer looked him in the eye. "I once stood in your place. And I too was...disrespectful. So might I offer you some advice?" Strange stared at him, nodding. "Forget everything you think you know."

"Uh...all right." *This is all a bunch of hocus-pocus*, Strange thought. But what choice did he have? He needed answers.

Inside, incense burned and the sun filtered

through screened walls. "The sanctuary of our teacher," his rescuer said. "The Ancient One."

"The Ancient One?" Strange echoed. "What's his real name?"

The other man just looked at him.

"Right," Strange said. "Forget everything I think I know. I'm sorry." He stepped farther into the room. An older Asian man sat reading. Strange nodded at him. "Thank you for...oh!" Two women appeared from nowhere and took off his coat. "Okay, that's, uh...a thing," he said. "Thank you. Hello."

A white-robed woman with a shaved head brought him tea. "Thank you," he said again to her. Then he looked back to the seated man. "Uh, thank you, Ancient One...for seeing me."

"You're very welcome," answered the woman in the white robe.

Confused, Strange looked back at his rescuer. "The Ancient One," he said.

"Thank you, Master Mordo," she said to him. So that was his name. "Thank you, Master Hamir!" she added to the seated man. Everyone spent a lot of time thanking one another here.

She turned back to him. "Mister Strange."

"Doctor, actually," he said, and sipped his tea.

"Well, no. Not anymore, surely." She smiled at him. "Isn't that why you're here? You've undergone many procedures. Seven, right?"

How did she know that? "Yeah," he said. Feeling like he should say something else, maybe something thankful, he added, "Good tea."

She went to a low table and began to make more tea. Strange decided to get to the point. "Did you heal a man named Pangborn? A paralyzed man."

"In a way," she said. Mordo watched the conversation with a quiet intentness from a few feet away.

"You helped him to walk again."

She kept smiling. "Yes."

Impossible, Strange thought. But he was here, so

43

he kept asking questions. "How do you correct a complete C7–C8 spinal cord injury?"

"Oh, I didn't correct it," she said, as though he had chosen the wrong word. "He couldn't walk; I convinced him that he could."

"You're not suggesting it was psychosomatic?" Strange had seen the images. Pangborn's spinal cord was completely severed.

"When you reattach a severed nerve, is it you who heals it back together or the body?"

"It's the cells," Strange said.

She nodded as if he were a bright student giving an expected answer. "And the cells are only programmed to put themselves together in very specific ways."

"That's right."

"What if I told you that your own body could be convinced to put itself back together in all sorts of ways?" she asked.

Now they were getting somewhere. "You're

talking about cellular regeneration," Strange said. "That's…bleeding-edge medical tech. Is that why you're working here, without a governing medical board?" He wanted to see her lab, read her research. "I mean…just how experimental is your treatment?"

With an even broader smile, she said simply, "Quite."

"So, you figured out a way to reprogram nerve cells to self-heal?" Strange couldn't believe what he was hearing. This was Nobel Prize–level innovation, if it was real.

"No, Mister Strange," she said, suddenly serious. "I know how to reorient the spirit to better heal the body."

"Spirit…to heal the body." So it was hocus-pocus. But…he'd seen the results with his own eyes. He'd seen Pangborn playing basketball. He had to give this a chance even though it went against everything he had ever learned. "Huh.

All…all right. How do we do that? Where do we start?"

The Ancient One held an open book up in front of him, displaying an image of the human body with its chakras, mystical energy points. Strange stared, trying to keep his shock in check, at least to start. "Don't like that map?" she asked when she saw his skeptical expression.

"Oh…no," he said. "It's…it's very good. It's just…you know, I've seen it before. In gift shops." Strange thought chakras were one of the goofy ideas scam artists used to separate sick people from their money.

She laughed and turned the page to another diagram. "And what about this one?"

"Acupuncture, great." Another scam as far as Strange could tell.

"Yeah? What about…that one?" She turned the page and Strange couldn't help it. He rolled his eyes. "You're showing me an MRI scan? I cannot believe this." If this "Ancient One" believed that magnetic resonance imaging was the same as chakras and acupuncture, Strange was wasting his time.

"Each of those maps was drawn up by someone who could see in part, but not the whole," she said.

The whole show was too much. Strange was tired, desperate, not to mention still frightened and in pain from the mugging. He started to raise his voice, letting all pretense of respect fall. "I spent my last dollar getting here on a one-way ticket, and you're talking to me about healing through belief?"

"You're a man who's looking at the world through a keyhole, and you spent your whole life trying to widen that keyhole," she answered, her tone still level and calm. "To see more, know more. And now, on hearing that it can be widened in ways you can't imagine, you reject the possibility?"

"No, I reject it because I do not believe in fairy tales about chakras or energy or the power of belief," he sneered. "There is no such thing as spirit! We are made of matter, and nothing more. We're just another tiny, momentary speck within an indifferent universe."

She still didn't seem bothered by his insulting tone. "You think too little of yourself," she said.

"Oh, you think you see through me, do you? Well, you don't. But I see through you!" Furious, he stabbed a finger at her . . . and then she did react.

She caught his wrist, turned his arm, and thrust a palm into the center of his chest. Something happened. He felt a wrenching sense of dislocation, and for a moment he was outside himself, looking at his own body from across the room. He held up his hands and saw a strange glow around them, trailing wisps of light. The Ancient One held her hand still for a moment, then curled her fingers. Strange felt a tug, and a moment later the vision had passed. He twitched, feeling his body again. "What did you just do to me?"

"I pushed your astral form out of your physical

form," she said, as if it was a perfectly ordinary thing to do.

She'd drugged him. That was it. That was part of their game here. "What's in that tea? Psilocybin? LSD?"

"Just tea," she said calmly. "With a little honey."

He couldn't help himself. He believed her. Or at least he was starting to. Was there some truth to all this mumbo jumbo? He'd felt it. He'd felt himself outside his body. "What just happened?"

"For a moment, you entered the Astral Dimension," she explained. "A place where the soul exists apart from the body."

"Why are you doing this to me?" Strange asked. He didn't care about Astral Dimensions. He wanted his hands back.

"To show you just how much you don't know," she said. "Open your eye."

For a moment he thought she was just giving him more mystical advice, but then everything around him changed. Strange was hurled up and out of Kamar-Taj, into the sky, above the clouds. He screamed, terrified by what he saw around him. He could see the curve of Earth and the bright-blue layer of the atmosphere against the infinite black of space. "This isn't real it isn't real it isn't—" Suddenly, in front of him, there was a butterfly. A beautiful monarch, wings gently working. Transfixed, Strange reached to touch it... then he was flung away again, down some kind of wormhole. Colors and swirls of energy whirlpooled around him. The world was coming apart in his head.

Somewhere in his mind, Strange heard Mordo's voice. "His heart rate is getting dangerously high."

Then he fell back into his body to find The Ancient One studying his face and putting a calming hand on his shoulder. "He looks all right to me," she said. Panting, Strange started to feel relieved that it was over. Then she took her hand and everything splintered again.

"You think you know how the world works?" She spoke in his mind as Strange tumbled through a shifting landscape of incredible shapes and colors. Were those cells? Were they worlds? He could not tell. He felt his body come apart and come back together, once, twice, a thousand times in the blink of an eye. "You think that this material universe is all there is? What is real? What mysteries lie beyond the reach of your senses? At the root of existence, mind and matter meet. Thoughts shape reality." Everything shifted again as he fell through a giant, staring eye into a vast space filled with crystal structures. Far away he saw other versions of himself, staring and frightened. "This universe is only one of an infinite number. Worlds without end. Some benevolent and life-giving..." He began to fall toward one world. "Others filled with malice and hunger. Dark places, where powers older than time lie, ravenous...and waiting." The world was not a world. It was a face, with eyes full of power and hate. Strange started to scream as it saw him…and then it was gone. Light surrounded him; he blazed across the emptiness again, faster and faster. "Who are you in this vast Multiverse, Mister Strange?"

He crashed back into the world. Actually crashed, falling from the ceiling of the Kamar-Taj sanctuary and smashing a chair. "Have you seen that before in a gift shop?" The Ancient One asked as he trembled on the floor. Her voice was gentle, but her meaning was clear.

Slowly, Strange got himself up to his knees. He held his hands out to her, shaking and over-whelmed. Now he believed. He had seen it. He had felt it. Mordo was right. He was ready to for-get what he had thought he knew. "Teach me," he begged.

For a long moment she looked at him.

Then, softly, she said, "No."

Mordo dragged Strange to the door and threw

him out into the street. The door shut. Strange banged on it, not caring about the searing pain in his hands. "No! No, no, no! Open the door! Please!"

But no one answered.

CHAPTER 4

Inside Kamar-Taj, The Ancient One consulted with some of her fellow Masters of the mystic arts. The debate was calm, but clearly the group had strong opinions.

Many came seeking Kamar-Taj. Few found it. Even fewer were worth learning its secrets... and even fewer of those were worthy of the teaching she could offer. That was why she wished to consult—there was often wisdom in other perspectives. But now the conversation was over. "Thank you, Masters," she said as they vanished through portals back to their homes away from Kamar-Taj. She could feel Mordo watching her. "You think I'm wrong to cast him out?"

"Five hours later, he's still on your doorstep," Mordo said. "There's a strength to him."

"Stubbornness, arrogance, ambition…" The Ancient One stood at a pedestal. A small instrument set atop it gave her a view of the different planes of reality, projected as a fiery globe above her. "I've seen it all before."

Mordo knew what she was thinking. "He reminds you of Kaecilius?"

"I cannot lead another gifted student to power, only to lose him to the darkness," The Ancient One said.

"You didn't lose me," Mordo pointed out. "I wanted the power to defeat my enemies. You gave me the power to defeat my demons. And to live within the natural law."

"We never lose our demons, Mordo. We only learn to live above them."

He understood the warning in her words. As soon as one started to believe demons were defeated, one stopped looking for them. He decided to change the subject. "Kaecilius still has the stolen pages. If he deciphers them, he could bring ruin upon us all. There may be dark days ahead. Perhaps...Kamar-Taj could use a man like Strange."

"Don't shut me out," Strange begged. "I have nowhere else to go." He said it over and over, and no one answered. Eventually, he sank down and sat, back to the door. He was done.

Just then, the door opened and Mordo hauled

him inside. Strange scrambled to his feet. "Thank you," he said, on the verge of tears. Without a word, Mordo led him through the temple to a room. It was dim and small, but clean, and Strange felt something he wasn't used to feeling: gratitude. "Thank you," he said again, not just to be polite. The Ancient One's vision had shaken something loose in him. He was seeing things he had never seen before. He had hope.

"Bed," Mordo said as he lit a stick of incense to freshen up the room's musty air. "Rest. Meditate... if you can. The Ancient One will send for you."

He handed Strange a slip of paper with the word *Shamballa* written on it.

"Uh, what's this? My mantra?"

"The Wi-Fi password," Mordo said from the door. He cracked a smile, just barely. "We're not savages."

Wi-Fi, Strange thought. He could contact Christine, tell her what he had seen. Looking at the watch she had given him when they were together, he turned it over. It was all he had left from the day he'd left New York. It was all he had left from his time with her. On the back was her inscription: TIME WILL TELL HOW MUCH I LOVE YOU.

He set the watch down. *Time*, he thought. He wanted to talk to her, but for one of the few times in his life, he wasn't sure what to say. He was still thinking about it when The Ancient One called for him and began his studies.

"The language of the mystic arts is as old as civilization," she began. They were kneeling, facing each other in her study. "The sorcerers of antiquity called the use of this language *spells*. But if that word offends your modern sensibilities, you can call it a program." With a gesture she drew a line of energy in the air, bright-orange and sparking. The line rotated, opening into a circle. She flicked her wrist and a square appeared around the circle, then smaller circles in its corners. "The source code that shapes reality. We harness energy drawn from other dimensions of the Multiverse, to cast spells, conjure shields and weapons to make magic." The center circle began to turn, as if the entire figure was not just a symbol but a magical machine of some kind. With a small push, she made the floating symbol expand into three dimensions, bulging toward Strange. He watched, astonished. Then she let it fall away.

"But...even if my fingers could do that, my hands would just be waving in the air. I mean, how do I get from here to there?"

"How did you get to reattach severed nerves, and put a human spine back together bone by bone?"

"Study and practice. Years of it."

From her look he understood that he had just

answered his own question. *Study and practice*, Strange thought. He could do that.

The first thing she did was turn him loose in Kamar-Taj's library. Strange read what she suggested, and that led him to other books. When he had finished one armload, he brought them back to the library and got more. The second time he made the trip, a blocky Asian man stood at a reading table near the library entrance. Behind him was another door, magically guarded. Strange didn't know what was on the other side, but he hoped to find out soon.

"Hey," he said, and set the books down.

The librarian—that's what Strange figured he must be—looked up. "Mister Strange," he said.

That was weird, how everyone knew him here

even though he didn't know any of them. "Uh…
Stephen, please. And you are?"

"Wong."

"Wong," Strange repeated. "Just Wong?" Wong
did not look impressed at his joke. Strange tried
another single-named person. "Or… Aristotle." Still
no reaction.

Wong waited for Strange to run out of steam.
Then he turned his attention to the books. *"The
Book of the Invisible Sun. Astronomia Nova. Codex
Imperium. Key of Solomon.* You finished all of
this?"

"Yup," Strange said. He was a fast reader, and a
fast learner.

After another long, considering look, Wong said,
"Come with me."

Strange followed him into another part of the
library. "This section is for Masters only. But at my
discretion, others may use it." He pulled a book

from the shelf. "We should start with *Maxim's Primer*. How is your Sanskrit?"

"I'm fluent in online translators."

Wong handed him the book. "Read it. Classical Sanskrit."

Strange saw a row of books high on the wall. Each had a sigil on the cover that glowed with power. "What are those?"

"The Ancient One's private collection."

"So they're forbidden?"

"No knowledge in Kamar-Taj is forbidden. Only certain practices. Those books are far too advanced for anyone other than the Sorcerer Supreme."

Strange went to the books and opened one. He did not understand the alphabet it was written in, let alone the language. It had fallen open to a gap where he could see pages torn out. "This one's got pages missing."

"That's *The Book of Cagliostro*. The study of time.

One of the rituals was stolen by a former Master. A Zealot called Kaecilius. Just after he strung up the former librarian and relieved him of his head." Wong paused for that to sink in. Then he took another book from a nearby shelf. "I'm now the guardian of these books. So if a volume from this collection should be stolen again, I'd know it. And you'd be dead before you ever left the compound." His point made, he handed the book to Strange.

"What if it's just overdue? You know? Any… late fees I should know about? Maybe, perhaps, um…" He gave up. "You know, people used to think that I was funny."

Still completely deadpan, Wong said, "Did they work for you?"

Ouch, Strange thought. "All right." He gathered up the stack of books Wong had chosen for him. "Well, it's been lovely talking to you—thank you for the books and for the horrifying story and for the threat upon my life."

Kaecilius and his Zealots stood in the sanctuary of a London cathedral. He unfolded a leather case containing the pages he had taken from *The Book of Cagliostro* and selected one showing an ominous rune. He and the Zealots all had the same rune on their foreheads now, a symbol of their devotion to their task. "Now we receive the power to destroy the one who betrayed us," Kaecilius said as he set the page on the floor. He drew the rune in the air above it, bloodred and pulsing. "The one who betrays the world."

When he had completed the rune, he and the Zealots chanted the ritual, repeating the phrase of power that would draw the dark being whose rune they watched, and tell him they were devoted to him. Across the barrier between his world and the Dark Dimension, Kaecilius felt a response.

Power flowed through him, and the floor around the page began to fold itself into a mystical pattern. He looked up and swept his arms through gestures he had learned from The Ancient One— gestures that he would soon use to destroy her. The cathedral's walls and stained-glass windows folded and twisted into new shapes, strange geometries no human had ever seen. *Yes*, Kaecilius thought. The ritual was working. Dormammu had heard their call for aid, and answered.

CHAPTER 5

Mordo and Wong walked among the trainees as they worked through exercises designed to develop the basic powers that were common to all magical orders. Strange had learned the gestures, but he could not create the lines of energy that seemed to come so easily to the other apprentices. None of the others helped him—Stephen Strange was still not used to asking for help from his peers.

After the exercises, Mordo brought out a case and

opened it, revealing rows of two-finger rings. "Mastery of the sling ring is essential to the mystic arts," he said as each student took one. They fit over the index and middle fingers, with a flat surface like half a set of brass knuckles. "They allow us to travel throughout the Multiverse." The students began to create crackling orange portals, but again Strange made the motions and got nothing, only a few sparks.

Mordo stopped next to him. Strange concentrated harder. "All you need to do is focus," Mordo said. "Visualize. See the destination in your mind. Look beyond the world in front of you. Imagine every detail. The clearer the picture, the quicker and easier the gateway will come." All around him, apprentices were forming their gateways, sharp and clear. Strange could barely make a spark appear. He wasn't going to quit, but he was getting too frustrated to focus.

"And stop," Mordo said as The Ancient One stepped out of the temple to the edge of the training ground. Another Master walked with her, hands folded into the loose sleeves of his robe. Strange recognized him, but they hadn't spoken yet.

"I'd like a moment alone with Mister Strange," she said.

"Of course." Mordo beckoned the other students to follow him inside the temple, leaving Strange alone with The Ancient One and her companion.

"My hands," Strange said, guessing she was going to criticize his lack of progress.

"It's not about your hands."

"How is this not about my hands?" he asked. They were all using their hands to make the symbols, weren't they? He had done all the reading his peers had, and more—it had to be his hands holding him back.

"Master Hamir," The Ancient One said. Her companion spread his hands…no, hand. His left arm ended in a scarred stump above the wrist. Without a word, Master Hamir used what remained of his left arm to draw a symbol of power in the air. He held it for a moment, then let it flicker away.

"Thank you, Master Hamir." He bowed and walked silently back into the temple. The Ancient One turned to Strange to drive home the lesson. "You cannot beat a river into submission. You have to surrender to its current, and use its power as your own."

"I...I control it by surrendering control? That doesn't make any sense."

"Not everything does," she said. "Not everything has to. Your intellect has taken you far in life. But it will take you no further. Surrender, Stephen." She raised her hands and he saw a sling ring on the left. With a quick circular gesture, she drew a portal in the air. "Silence your ego and your power will rise. Come with me." Stunned, Strange followed The Ancient One through the portal.

They emerged onto a mountainside. Wind howled and snow swept over them. It was freezing, colder than anything Strange had ever felt. The air was thin in his lungs. He couldn't draw a whole breath, and what air he managed to get stung his nose and throat. "Wait," he said. "Is this..."

"Everest. It's beautiful." She was looking out over the Himalayas, "the Roof of the World," seemingly unaffected by the wind or the cold.

"Yeah, you're right. Beautiful," he said. "It's freezing, but...beautiful."

"At this temperature, a person can last for thirteen minutes before suffering permanent loss of function," The Ancient One said like she was reading from a guidebook.

"Great." Strange wondered what the point of this lesson was. He looked where she was looking. It was an amazing view, yes. But again, what was the point? Surely she didn't bring him all the way here just to play tour guide.

"But you will likely go into shock within the first two minutes," she added.

"What?" He started to turn back to her.

"Surrender, Stephen," she said in a singsong tone as she passed through the portal back to Kamar-Taj and closed it behind her.

"No, no! Don't!" He tried to dive through it but only crashed down onto the snow-covered ground. Now also covered in snow, Strange felt more than cold—he felt angry and desperate.

Back in the training courtyard, The Ancient One waited. Mordo saw her and approached. "How is our new recruit?"

"We shall see," she said. "Any second now."

"No, not again." Mordo had seen her do this before. It was a difficult test, and those who did not pass...he took a step forward. "Maybe I should..." he suggested helpfully.

She stopped him. He saw she held one hand behind her back, flicking a fan open and closed. It was her one nervous habit, or at least the only one Mordo had ever observed, and even then, he would hesitate to call her nervous the same way other people got nervous. They waited...and waited...

A portal sparked to life in the courtyard and Strange fell through it, gasping. Ice crusted his beard. He weakly got to his hands and knees and looked up at The Ancient One. His face was a whirlwind of emotion—slowly receding fear, and anger again. But eventually, in his face she saw that he was beginning to understand.

Alone in his room, Strange relived the experience. The panic, the desperation...and then the incredible moment when he had felt it happen. He had made the portal.

He had made magic! Up until recently he hadn't even believed in magic, but he had created a portal for himself just the same.

Behind him hung a new robe. He would wear the gray of the apprentice no longer. Now that he had shown the first glimmerings of power, he had a new, deep-red robe. And he decided he needed a new appearance to go with it.

He hadn't shaved or had a haircut since leaving New York, weeks before. Now, by the light of a single bulb, he cut his own hair, taking his time. He had nowhere to be. His hands hurt but for some reason, now that he knew he could do something wonderful again, they didn't seem to hurt as much. With a borrowed electric razor, he clipped his beard and then shaved it to a shape that suited him. He liked the sharpness it gave his face. He combed his hair straight back, then considered himself in the mirror. Yes. He was a new man. He had come seeking wisdom, and he'd begun to find it.

Now it was time to see what else he could learn.

CHAPTER 6

Stephen," Wong said when he saw Strange come into the library.

Strange nodded. "Wong."

Wong saw something new in Strange, and looked at him with some suspicion. "What do you want?"

"Books on astral projection."

"You're not ready for that," Wong said.

"Try me," Strange taunted. Wong said nothing.

"Come on. Do you ever laugh?" Still nothing. "Oh...come on, just give me the book, huh?"

Wong didn't even bother to shake his head. "No."

So Strange took matters into his own hands.

If Wong wasn't going to give him the books, he would just have to take them. If he could get good enough at creating portals, then he could pop one open and slip a book out while Wong was looking the other way.

Strange practiced obsessively. Because of his dedication—and soaring confidence—he got good at this, fast. He absorbed everything he could from the books Wong had tried to stop him from reading. He was so devoted that he started astrally projecting himself to read while his body slept. There was so much to learn; he couldn't spare the time to just lie in his bed uselessly.

After a few days of this blistering pace, The Ancient One called him into her study. "Once, in this room, you begged me to let you learn. Now

I'm told you question every lesson, preferring to teach yourself."

"Once, in this room, you told me to open my eyes," Strange shot back. "Now I'm being told to blindly accept rules that make no sense."

"Like the rule against conjuring a gateway in the library?"

Uh-oh, Strange thought. He'd thought Wong hadn't noticed. "Wong told on me?"

"You're advancing quickly with your sorcery skills," The Ancient One said. "You need a safe space to practice your spells."

She reached out a hand, and when she made a small gesture, the air in the middle of the study seemed to fracture into a thousand shards that hung tinkling in space. Each of them reflected part of reality at a different angle. She walked toward this wall and through it. Strange followed.

"You are now inside the Mirror Dimension," she said. "Ever-present, but undetected." Outside, the other apprentices and sorcerers in the study went about their business. Strange and The Ancient One were completely invisible to them. "The real world isn't affected by what happens here. We use the Mirror Dimension to train, surveil, and sometimes to contain threats. You don't want to be stuck in here without your sling ring."

"Hold on. Sorry, what do you mean, threats?"

With a thrusting motion The Ancient One folded the matter of the ceiling, creating a concentric pattern of timbers with a black opening in the middle. Strange sensed spaces beyond, as if she had folded reality out of the way to make room for... something else. "Learning of an infinite Multiverse included learning of infinite dangers," she said. "And if I told you everything else that you don't already know, you'd run from here in terror."

And she would say no more. She had made her point, though. Seeing the way she could so easily manipulate reality told Strange there was still much he didn't know. He would have to train even harder.

Later, outside, Strange and Mordo prepared for physical training. Learning martial arts was part of body discipline, just as learning sorcery was discipline for the mind. "So, just how ancient is she?" Strange asked. The Ancient One, flicking her fan, was watching two other students as they sparred.

"No one knows the age of the Sorcerer Supreme," Mordo said. "Only that she is Celtic and never talks about her past."

"You follow her even though you don't know?" Strange found this hard to believe. How could anyone trust a leader who kept those kinds of secrets?

"I know that she's steadfast, but unpredictable. Merciless, yet kind. She made me what I am."

Mordo dropped into a fighting stance. Strange did, too. "Trust your teacher," Mordo said as they began to circle each other. "And don't lose your way."

"Like Kaecilius?" Strange asked.

Mordo lunged at Strange. They exchanged punches at practice speed, testing each other's defenses. "That's right," Mordo said.

Strange grappled with him, locking his arms and buying himself a second of time to reassess the fight. "You knew him."

Twisting out of Strange's hold, Mordo spun him around and got Stephen in a firm choke hold. Strange gripped Mordo's arm and struggled to free himself, wiggling his body to gain leverage where he could, but he couldn't break Mordo's hold. "When he first came to us, he'd lost everyone he ever loved," Mordo growled in Strange's ear. He was suddenly intense and angry. "He was a grieving and broken man, searching for answers in the mystic arts. A brilliant student, but he was proud, headstrong. Questioned The Ancient One, rejected our teaching."

Ah, Strange thought. Mordo was warning him because he thought Strange was following the same path. Well, he had some surprises in store for those who thought they could possibly predict Stephen Strange.

He let go of Mordo's arm and pounded an elbow back into Mordo's gut. Taking his opportunity to wrest free, Stephen spun away, feeling his throat. Mordo didn't come after him. "He left Kamar-Taj." Mordo panted. "His disciples followed him like sheep seduced by false doctrine."

"He stole the forbidden ritual, right?"

"Yes."

"What did it do?" Strange had gotten the sense that the ritual was important, but nobody in Kamar-Taj seemed to be doing anything about it.

He saw The Ancient One watching him from near the temple door, and wondered what she thought she saw in him.

"No more questions." Mordo went to a rack at the edge of the training ground and selected a short carved wooden staff.

"What's that?" Strange asked.

"That's a question," Mordo said with the smallest of smiles. *A joke*, Strange thought. He was starting to like Mordo. "This is a relic," Mordo went on. He pointed the staff at Strange, then turned his wrist to hold it parallel to the ground. "Some magic is too powerful to sustain, so we imbue objects with it. Allowing them to take the strain we cannot. This is the Staff of the Living Tribunal." He gripped it with both hands and it flared with magical energy as he struck the ground, making Strange flinch. "There are many relics. The Wand of Watoomb. The Vaulting Boots of Valtorr." As he said the last, he kicked his feet together. A tiny magical sigil came to life in the air near his feet, then faded away.

"They just roll off the tongue, don't they?" Strange commented. Mordo grinned. "When do I get my relic?"

"When you're ready."

"I think I'm ready." Strange was getting tired of people telling him he wasn't ready for things. Wong had said the same thing about books, but he'd been wrong, hadn't he? Strange had mastered astral projection with basically no problems—a few setbacks didn't warrant Wong's refusal to help. He could handle a relic, too.

"You're ready when the relic decides you're ready," Mordo said, still smiling. "For now, conjure a weapon."

Strange held both hands in front of him and, with some effort, brought forth a bar of energy between them. Without warning, Mordo struck it with the staff. Strange absorbed the shock and barely got braced to deflect Mordo's next strike. "Fight!" Mordo shouted as they sparred. "Fight like your life depended on it!"

He launched himself into the air, taking three long strides past Strange on the Vaulting Boots of Valtorr—and then swinging himself around to drop Strange with a kick to the chest. Looming over Strange, Mordo was suddenly all business. "Because one day it may."

In the evenings, Strange had some time to reflect on what he had learned during the day, or to study, depending on how the mood struck him. Or to think of all he had left behind. Tonight he was thinking about Christine. He opened his laptop and started to type her a message.

Christine

I'm e-mailing you one more time to

Then he stopped. To what? He had already e-mailed her twice, and she hadn't answered. What else could he say? Someday, he vowed, he would apologize to her face-to-face. She deserved it...and the longer Strange was apart from her, the more he realized how much he missed her.

Someday, he thought again, looking at the watch on the table next to the laptop. He would make it right. They would have a future together.

Future.

CHAPTER 7

Future...That got him thinking—about all the mistakes he had made along the way to Kamar-Taj. Wong had said *The Book of Cagliostro* was devoted to the study of time. Strange had been too proud back in New York to admit any of his mistakes, but now in Kamar-Taj his head was clearer. He was learning a little bit about being humble. What if he could undo his mistakes? What if...?

He went to the library late that night and took

down *The Book of Cagliostro* from its place on the high shelf. Strange realized that his study had paid off. He could understand the script in *The Book of Cagliostro* now, when it had just seemed like random marks the first time he opened it. Sitting at a table, he began to read, taking bites from an apple as he turned the pages—he always found new research to be hungry work. He saw symbols and sigils on the pages that he recognized from artifacts in the library—specifically the artifact sitting on a pedestal not ten feet from where he sat.

The Eye of Agamotto.

"Wong?" he called out.

No answer. He was alone in the library. *No knowledge in Kamar-Taj is forbidden*, Wong had said. *Only certain practices.*

He was about to test the truth of that statement.

Strange went to the pedestal and detached the Eye of Agamotto from its fixture. He hung it around his neck and returned to the book. "Okay," he muttered to himself. "First, open the Eye of Agamotto."

He touched the middle and ring fingers of both hands together, then moved them in a circle. The Eye of Agamotto opened, radiating green light.

"All right," Strange said. So far, so good.

He spread the fingers of both hands and rotated them, creating a circle of green light with runic symbols in its center. The shape was just as big as his spread hand, and when he turned his hand, it turned as well. Bands of green energy circled his right forearm, rotating around his wrist of their own accord.

He held the circle out toward the half-eaten apple. When he turned it clockwise, some more of the apple disappeared. Future bites that he had not yet taken. The relic's power was carrying the apple forward into the future while Strange stayed in the present. He turned the circle counterclockwise, and the bites disappeared, restoring the apple chunk by chunk. The apple was whole again, even though he could still taste the bites he had taken from it.

"Oh my," he breathed. It was real.

He could manipulate time.

He turned the circle clockwise again, further this time. The apple turned into a core and then began to decay, right there on the table. Strange restored it and looked back to the book. He turned to the place where pages had been ripped out of the book. Slowly, he turned the green circle of power counterclockwise, this time directing it at the book . . . and the missing pages reappeared. Now—finally—he would be able to discover what the missing ritual did, since no one in Kamar-Taj would tell him.

A large red symbol occupied much of the right-hand page, and the facing page showed a set of circular symbols. Around them was the text of a new ritual. Strange studied it, trying to understand.

"Dormammu," Strange read. "The Dark Dimension. Eternal life?"

Now he understood how The Ancient One had lived so long. She must be tapping into this Dark Dimension...but beyond his questions of how, the revelation shocked him. Could it be true? Was there another explanation that he was missing? He had gotten the sense that The Ancient One was a force for good in the world, and her associating with something as dangerous as this...Strange had a hard time focusing on that question with the new sensations blazing through his mind. Swept away by the power he felt, and the idea of even vaster power contained in the ritual, he began to turn the ring....

With a soft chiming sound, crystal structures appeared in the air over the table. They were like the Mirror Dimension portal, only larger, stronger—as if the dimension they marked had to be held back by greater power. Strange concentrated, and began to feel the portal open.

"Stop!" someone shouted. The crystalline portal

vanished and Strange lost his hold on the green circle. It, too, disappeared.

He looked up to see Wong furiously coming toward him from another part of the library. "Tampering with the continuum of probability is forbidden!" he said, almost shouting. It was by far the loudest Strange had ever seen Wong get.

"I...I was just doing exactly what it said in the book," he protested.

"And what did the book say about the dangers of performing that ritual?"

He didn't have an answer for that. "I don't know. I hadn't gotten to that part yet." As he admitted this, Strange started to realize that he might have overreached. He maybe should have been a little more careful.

Mordo appeared at his other side, seemingly out of nowhere. "Temporal manipulations can create branches in time. Unstable dimensional openings. Spatial paradoxes! Time loops!" he shouted. "You want to get stuck reliving the same moment over and over, forever—or never having existed at all?"

Strange knew he was in the wrong. "They really should put the warnings *before* that stuff," he said quietly, trying to lighten the situation up a little.

Wong wasn't having any of it. "Your curiosity could have gotten you killed. You weren't manipulating the space-time continuum; you were wrecking it." He snapped *The Book of Cagliostro* shut and carried it back to its place. "We do not tamper with natural law. We defend it."

As Wong put the book away, Mordo studied Strange. "How did you learn to do that? Where did you learn the litany of spells required to even understand it?"

"I've got a photographic memory," Strange said. "It's how I got my MD and PhD at the same time."

"What you just did takes more than a good memory. You were born for the mystic arts." Mordo was looking at Strange in a new way. There was anger still, but also some respect...and maybe even a little fear.

Strange nodded, taking the compliment, but it didn't make him feel better. "And yet, my hands still shake."

"For now, yes," Wong said.

Strange felt a glimmer of hope. "Not forever?"

"We're not prophets," Mordo said.

Fine, Strange thought. But that wasn't good enough. If he was born for the mystic arts, it was about time someone told him what the mystic arts were for. "When do you start telling me *what* we are?"

Wong and Mordo exchanged a look. Then Wong spoke while he walked to the Eye of Agamotto's pedestal. He rotated the pedestal and the glowing globe of Earth appeared in the air above it. "While heroes like the Avengers protect the world from physical dangers, we sorcerers safeguard it against more mystical threats. The Ancient One is the latest in a long line of Sorcerers Supreme, going back thousands of years to the father of the mystic arts, the mighty Agamotto. The same sorcerer who created the Eye you so recklessly borrowed."

"Agamotto built three Sanctums in places of power, where great cities now stand." Wong pointed to three doorways, inscribed with large symbols, in the wall behind the Eye's pedestal. "That door leads to the Hong Kong Sanctum, that door to the New York Sanctum. That one, to the London Sanctum." On the globe, the three symbols appeared, and lines of power grew to connect them. "Together, the Sanctums generate a protective shield around our world."

"The Sanctums protect the world," Mordo added, "and we sorcerers protect the Sanctums."

There was an obvious gap in what they were telling him, Strange thought. "From what?"

"Other-dimensional beings that threaten our universe," Wong said.

"Like Dormammu?"

Again, Mordo and Wong looked at each other. "Where did you learn that name?" Mordo asked.

"I just read it in *The Book of Cagliostro*. Why?"

Wong rotated the top of the pedestal again, and again the scene shifted. The lights of Earth went out. "Dormammu dwells in the Dark Dimension. Beyond time." The globe continued to spin, revealing a huge hole in its surface. Through it they saw an infinite space filled with corrupted worlds, and rippling with dark energies. "He is the cosmic conqueror, the destroyer of worlds," Wong went on. "A being of infinite power and endless hunger on a quest to invade every universe and bring all worlds into his Dark Dimension. And he hungers for Earth most of all."

Strange was starting to put two and two together. "The pages that Kaecilius stole..."

Wong nodded. "A ritual to contact Dormammu and draw power from the Dark Dimension."

"*Uhhh* . . . okay." Strange chuckled at how insane that sounded. He could accept a lot, but there were limits to everything. "Okay. I'm out. I . . . I came here to heal my hands, not to fight in some mystical war."

Mordo and Wong both looked at him with disgust . . . and pity. Strange didn't care. He wasn't a soldier. He wasn't a guardian of Earth against interdimensional monsters. He was a doctor. And he wanted to be a doctor again.

Before either of the Masters broke their silence, the deep chiming of church bells rang in the library. Wong looked at one of the doors that seemed to be the source of the disturbance.

"London," he said.

The door burst open and a figure staggered through the portal beyond it, stumbling a few steps into the room before falling dead on the floor.

CHAPTER 8

Through the still-open portal, Strange saw a tall man wearing a sorcerer's tunic. His face was disfigured by some strange gray-and-purple decay around the eyes, but those eyes . . . they burned with power and hate.

"Kaecilius!" Wong shouted. "No!"

As the words left Wong's mouth, Kaecilius raised one hand. The air over his head glowed and a sphere of magical energy formed. Looking straight through the portal at them, he brought his hand down.

A fiery explosion blasted out through the library. Smoke and rubble crashed into the room, and the force of the explosion blew Strange through another door. He landed hard and rolled up against a wall, slamming his ribs against the stone. It was dark except for the glow of the portal he had just passed through...but even that flickered and disappeared as he got to his feet.

Where was he?

"Wong?" he called out. "Mordo?"

There was no answer. Strange walked through the darkness and found himself in a large room with a stairway leading up. There was faint glow here from dim lights set into the walls. Beyond the staircase was a door. Through its windows, Strange could see what looked like daylight. He walked toward the door, still feeling the effects of the explosion. He could be anywhere.

But when he pushed through the door, he saw an instantly familiar sight. Cars rolling slowly down a side street. Pedestrians walking and laughing. They looked at him with surprised expressions on their faces, and he remembered he was dressed in the robes of Kamar-Taj, and was completely out of place. He also still wore the Eye of Agamotto on its chain around his neck. Strange knew this place. Was it possible? He turned and saw the address plate on the front of the building: 177A BLEECKER STREET.

He was in New York City. Greenwich Village, to be exact. Strange took a step back and looked up. There, high on the building's facade, was the symbol of the New York Sanctum.

So, the explosion back in Kamar-Taj had blown him through the open portal to here. *There must be a Master here*, he thought. All three Sanctums were supposed to be guarded. He had to find whoever was in charge here and tell them what Kaecilius had done. London was under attack and Kamar-Taj was damaged, too. Strange wasn't sure how much time he had to get help.

Strange turned and went back into the Sanctum. He called out as he walked through the foyer toward the staircase. "Hello?" No answer.

He went upstairs and found himself in a room with three glass doorways. Through them he saw three different landscapes: From left to right, they were a dense forest, an open ocean, and a mountain he didn't recognize. He opened the center door and a salt breeze blew the hair back from his forehead. It also stung in the cuts on his face. This was a different kind of portal. Strange shut the door and saw a large knob set in a pedestal in the middle of the room, inscribed with symbols. He turned it and the vista through the door spun and changed. Now it was an arid desert.

He kept searching. Most of the top floor was

filled with cases displaying different artifacts, although Strange didn't recognize any of them from his considerable reading. A red cloak with an ornate collar hung in a tall glass case. It seemed to ripple as he approached. Odd. He looked at it for a long moment, wondering if it was a threat. "Hello?" he called again. Still, he heard nothing. *Am I alone here?*

As he formulated that thought, he heard the distinctive sound of folding matter from downstairs. Apparently, he wasn't alone any longer, if he ever was. From the top of the staircase, he saw Kaecilius and a pair of his Zealots enter through a portal. One of the Zealots was relatively slight, but her face seemed implacable. The other was enormous, and in any other company would have been the most intimidating member of the group. Facing them in the foyer was a Master whom Strange didn't recognize.

Kaecilius, however, did. "Daniel," he said, his voice full of surprise. "I see they made you Master of this Sanctum."

Daniel, Strange thought. *He must be Daniel Drumm.* That was a name he'd heard in conversations among the Masters at Kamar-Taj.

"Do you know what that means?" Drumm responded.

"That you'll die protecting it." There was respect in Kaecilius's voice. His disfigured face was serious as he created the translucent blade of a Space Shard between his hands. Drumm raised a shield as Kaecilius lunged. The Space Shard deflected off the shield, but weakened it. Drumm, creating a weapon of his own, struck back, but Kaecilius had tapped the power of Dormammu. He was much more powerful than even this Master could hope to become. He shattered Drumm's defenses and drove the blade of the Space Shard deep into Drumm's belly.

"Stop!" Strange shouted. He was halfway down the stairs, rushing to help Drumm.

Kaecilius spent a long moment looking at Strange. "How long have you been at Kamar-Taj, Mister ... ?"

"Doctor," Strange corrected him. He would put up with being Mister Strange to The Ancient One, but not this maniac.

Kaecilius looked puzzled. "Just Doctor?"

"It's Strange."

"Maybe," Kaecilius said, misunderstanding completely. "Who am I to judge?"

Strange couldn't believe that in the middle of all this destruction and death, they were stumbling over basic introductions and titles. Kaecilius, too, lost interest in the conversation. He jerked the Space Shard free of the dying Daniel Drumm and charged toward Strange.

Strange created a cable of energy between his hands. Kaecilius was running up the wall as if gravity had turned on its side just for him. At Kaecilius's command, the Zealots came after Strange, too, chasing him back into the interior of the Sanctum. He countered their attacks, striking with the energy whip he had conjured. Kaecilius threw the Space Shard like a spear, straight at Strange's head. At the last moment, Strange deflected it. It smashed into the wall, which splintered into a small version of a Mirror Dimension portal before disappearing.

Strange ran for the glass doors. He couldn't face Kaecilius and both Zealots on his own. Behind him, Kaecilius cast a spell, and the floor unfolded beneath Strange's feet. As fast as he ran, the glass doors got farther away and the Zealots drew closer. Strange turned to face them. He spawned two separate energy shields, just as Mordo had taught him.

One of them flickered out. Of course.

Kaecilius swung upside down and walked on the ceiling toward Strange. The Zealots were on the walls and the floor. Strange fought them off as best he could, striking one of them back down to the floor with the energy whip. Then Kaecilius folded and bent the entire room around him, spinning it so Strange tumbled from floor to wall to ceiling to wall. He had just gotten his feet under him again when Kaecilius tipped the space the other way. Strange found himself hanging from a window frame. Below him, Kaecilius's Zealots stood, waiting for him to fall.

One of them, the woman, stood directly in front of one of the glass doors. The center one, the one he had spun from ocean to desert. A heavy vase fell past him and smashed through the door. Other debris followed, scattering down the sloping sand dune on the other side.

Strange had an idea. It was a little crazy, but he didn't seem to have a choice. He let go and fell, hitting the Zealot with both feet and driving her through the door. She skidded and tumbled down an enormous dune, and he found he could stand again. Reality wasn't bent in the same direction here.

He got to his feet and reached for the knob in the center of the room, but as he did the other Zealot attacked. Strange grappled with him and desperately fought him off. He spun the knob and the desert landscape vanished, replaced by a steaming jungle. The slender Zealot was now trapped wherever the other side of the portal had been. Enraged, her fellow Zealot charged Strange, who used his own momentum against him. He got under the Zealot and flipped him through the air...and through the portal into the jungle. Quickly, he spun the knob again, revealing yet another landscape.

Even though Strange was elated by his victory, there was still Kaecilius.

The dark sorcerer created another pair of Space Shards, one for each hand, and came after Strange, his haunted eyes glowing with the energies of the Dark Dimension. Strange ran for the artifact gallery, creating another energy whip as he went. He grabbed a magic lantern of some kind and spun to face Kaecilius, who stopped and kept his distance, waiting to see what Strange would do next.

Then a smile spread over his ruined face. "You don't know how to use that, do you?"

"What?" Strange looked at the lantern. It was true. He had no idea what it was.

So he did the obvious thing. He swung it at Kaecilius, who batted it aside with the Space Shards and attacked again. Strange parried his attacks, but Kaecilius got him off balance and knocked him into one of the glass cases. Strange got up and Kaecilius easily knocked him down once again. Scrambling across the floor, getting desperate, Strange dodged the Space Shards one more time, only to have Kaecilius kick him backward into yet another glass case.

Then Kaecilius went for the kill—and over

Strange's head, a fold of something red shot out and tangled Kaecilius's arm. Kaecilius jerked free of it, but another fold blocked his next swing. He dragged Strange away from the case to the railing over the long drop to the foyer. Strange was too battered to defend himself. Kaecilius hit him once, twice, and a third heavy punch knocked Strange over the railing.

The red robe with the ornate collar flashed past Kaecilius and after Strange. The corrupted Master stood watching, puzzled...and a moment later, Doctor Strange rose into view again, wrapped in the cloak, the Eye of Agamotto shining on his chest. He felt a new power coursing through him. Was this what Mordo had meant about a relic choosing him?

If so, it was excellent timing. He braided another energy whip between his hands and snapped it out toward Kaecilius, who caught it on the blade of his Space Shard. Sparks of arcane energy showered the floor as Kaecilius struggled. Then he yanked on the Space Shard, and Strange flew past him to crash on the floor. He got up and the cloak dragged him backward. What was it doing? Kaecilius advanced.

Strange looked up and saw an ax in a bracket high on the wall. He went after it, but the cloak stopped him in his tracks, pulling backward. What was going on here? Weren't the artifacts supposed to help the Masters? Kaecilius sprang forward and the cloak itself lashed out at him, knocking him down. Still, it dragged Strange away from the ax. He tried to fight it, but it was too strong.

As he reeled backward, the cloak caught an odd framework in a shadowed corner and threw it toward Kaecilius. A moment later, Strange understood why. The framework wrapped itself around Kaecilius's arms and legs, binding him on his knees with his arms held behind him. The frame moved with a mechanical purpose, tightening everywhere it could. Then it completed its work, covering his mouth with a series of interlocking small plates. Kaecilius resisted only for a moment. Then, knowing he was trapped, he said something behind the plates.

Curious, Strange went to him and uncovered his mouth.

"You'll die here," Kaecilius said. He was calm, even serene.

"Oh, stop it," Strange said.

"You cannot stop this, Mister Doctor."

"Why—" Strange stopped himself. It wasn't worth correcting Kaecilius's mistake about his name. "Look, I don't even know what 'this' is," he said.

"It's the end and the beginning," Kaecilius said softly. "The many becoming the few, becoming the One."

Strange didn't have time for more mystical

ravings. He got enough of that back in Kamar-Taj. "Look, if you're not going to start making sense, I'm just going to have to put this thing back on."

"Tell me, Mister Doctor," Kaecilius began, and Strange lost his patience.

"All right, look. My name is Doctor Stephen Strange."

"You *are* a doctor." Kaecilius sounded surprised.

"Yes."

"A scientist," Kaecilius said. "You understand the laws of nature. All things age. All things die. In the end, our sun burns out, our universe grows cold and perishes. But the Dark Dimension ... it's a place beyond time."

"That's it," Strange said. He walked up to Kaecilius with the mouth covering. "I'm putting this thing back on."

"This world doesn't have to die, Doctor," Kaecilius said, more emphatically. Strange paused. "This world can take its rightful place among so many others, as part of the One. The great and beautiful One. And we can all live forever."

"Really?" Strange challenged him. "What do you have to gain out of this New Age dimensional utopia?"

"The same as you. The same as everyone. Life. Eternal life. People think in terms of good and evil, but really, time is the true enemy of us all. Time kills everything."

"What about the people you killed?" Strange shot back, thinking of Daniel Drumm lying dead at the bottom of the stairs.

Kaecilius couldn't shrug, but Strange had the feeling he would have. "Tiny, momentary specks within an indifferent universe," he said.

Wait, Strange thought. He remembered using exactly those words to The Ancient One, right after his arrival in Kamar-Taj. How had Kaecilius known that? Did he have ears inside Kamar-Taj?

Spies? Or was it just a coincidence? Or...some kind of message from a different power?

Kaecilius didn't say one way or the other. "Yes. You see, you see what we're doing? The world is not what it ought to be. Humanity longs for the eternal, for a world beyond time, because time is what enslaves us. Time is an insult. Death is an insult. Doctor...we don't seek to rule this world. We seek to save it, to hand it over to Dormammu, who is the intent of all evolution, the Why of all existence."

Now Kaecilius was revealing himself to be a fanatic. "The Sorcerer Supreme defends existence," Strange said.

Ignoring him, Kaecilius asked, "What was it that brought you to Kamar-Taj, Doctor? Was it enlightenment? Power? You came to be healed, as did we all. Kamar-Taj is a place that collects broken things. We all come with the promise of being healed, but instead The Ancient One gives us parlor tricks. The real magic she keeps for herself.

Have you ever wondered how she managed to live this long?"

"I...I saw the rituals in *The Book of Cagliostro*."

"So, you know." Kaecilius sounded satisfied. "The ritual gives me the power to overthrow The Ancient One and tear her Sanctums down, to let the Dark Dimension in. Because what The Ancient One hoards, Dormammu gives freely. Life, everlasting. He is not the destroyer of worlds, Doctor; he is the savior of worlds."

"No. I mean, come on. Look at your face," Strange said, hoping the obvious damage would be enough to at least give the fanatic some pause. "Dormammu made you a murderer. Just how good can his kingdom be?" Kaecilius smiled. Puzzled, Strange asked, "You think that's funny?"

Kaecilius's smile grew broader. "No, Doctor. What's funny is that you've lost your sling ring."

Strange looked down. It was true. His sling ring was gone.

Then he heard something from the bottom of the stairs. He turned and saw, too late, a Zealot coming out of a portal. In the next moment he felt the Zealot's Space Shard bury itself deep in his chest. All the strength went out of Strange's legs. Staggering, he tumbled down the stairs. Strange knew he was hurt badly. He could feel pressure building in his chest as blood pooled around his heart from the wound. He needed a doctor—now. There was no way he could fight the Zealot.

But still, the Zealot came after him, bringing another Space Shard into existence.

The red cloak came to his rescue, ripping itself away from Strange's body and wrapping around the Zealot's head. It dragged him off balance and flung him to the ground, doing its best to incapacitate the tough fanatic. For a piece of cloth, magical or no, the cloak was doing an astounding job and, from what Stephen could make out, seemed to be winning.

From one of its folds, Strange's sling ring bounced across the floor toward him. He snatched it up and tried to focus his fading energy on creating a portal. He knew where he had to go. The portal materialized. On the other side, he could see a broom closet. Yes. He staggered through.

Behind him, the Zealot still struggled against the cloak.

CHAPTER 9

A startled nurse saw Doctor Stephen Strange reel out of the broom closet into the hospital hall. He reeled even farther into the wall, leaving a bloody handprint. "Sir, can I help you?" the nurse said.

"Doctor Palmer," Strange panted. "Where is she?"

"Sir, we need to—"

"Where is she?" Strange shouted.

"At the nurses' station."

Strange pushed past her. He was in bad shape, and each second wasted could cost him. "Christine!"

She ran around the counter at the nurses' station. "Stephen? Oh my god. What—"

"We need to get me on an operating table *now*," he said. It was getting harder to draw breath. "Just you. Now! I haven't any time!"

Christine helped him through a swinging door into an emergency-room operating theater. She laid him on a table. "What happened?"

"Stabbed," he said. "Cardiac tamponade."

She started working, peeling back his robe to get a view of the wound. "What are you wearing?" That was a long story Strange didn't have time to tell. Christine tapped on his chest at various points. "The chest cavity is clear."

Now he really couldn't breathe. That fact on top of his pain made it nearly impossible for him to gasp out, "The blood...is in the pericardial sac."

Then he felt himself slipping away, felt his over-exerted hands relaxing and going limp. Dimly, he heard Christine saying, "No. No, no, no, no, no, no, no! Stephen! Stephen!"

As she yelled at her former friend, she was getting a syringe ready to draw the blood out of the pericardial sac around his heart. If it didn't happen fast, the blood would squeeze his heart and Strange would die. And it had to happen just right. Stephen felt himself losing touch with his body. In his last moment of consciousness, that gave him an idea, a last hope...

He heaved himself up and out of his body. Astral projection. His astral form hovered just above the table. He turned and saw his body on the table, with the ragged wound in his chest from the Zealot's Space Shard. Christine brought the needle to his chest, pausing. If she put it in the wrong place, it would draw blood out of the heart instead of from around it. That would be fatal.

Strange couldn't help himself. Even after all he'd learned at Kamar-Taj, he couldn't just let someone operate without giving his advice. "Just a little higher," he said.

Christine screamed and jumped away, covering her mouth with one gloved hand. Strange had forgotten that he was back in the normal world, where people didn't expect things like astral projection. "Please be careful with the needle."

"Stephen?" she squeaked. "Oh lord, oh lord. What am I seeing?"

"My astral body."

"Are you dead?"

"No, Christine, but I am dying." He tried to say it gently, but he was in a bit of a hurry.

"Right. Right." She gathered herself and rested the point of the needle against his skin. Strange showed her the exact spot, sinking his astral fingers into his body's chest.

"I've . . . I've never seen a wound like this before,"

she said. The skin around the wound was cracked and gray. Just like the skin around Kaecilius's eyes. The Space Shards were weapons of the Dark Dimension. "What were you stabbed with?"

"I don't know," Strange said. He watched her work, slowly drawing blood into the syringe. Then, out of the corner of his eye, he saw the astral form of one of the Zealots ghosting into the room. "I'm going to have to vanish now."

"No, I—"

"Keep me alive, will you?" Strange vanished from her sight and turned to face the Zealot. He was the one who had stabbed him. He must have astrally projected himself to escape the cloak... and to finish what he'd started back in the New York Sanctum.

The Zealot charged and crashed into Strange. They wrestled across the operating room, floating through delicate instruments, and battering each other as Christine kept slowly drawing blood from around Strange's heart. The Zealot was strong, and Strange hadn't learned enough martial arts to keep up with him. He was losing the fight. They tumbled over the operating table, jostling Christine a little. Astral bodies, despite their ghostlike appearances, could have small effects in the real world. Then they phased through the wall out into the hallway, through a vending machine where Doctor Nic West was just getting some potato chips. Several other candies fell to the bottom of the machine when Strange and the Zealot passed through it. Doctor West scooped them all up—*What a lucky day for Nic*, Strange noted bitterly.

The Zealot was still getting the better of Strange, landing blow after blow. After one stunning punch, Strange felt his astral link to his body slipping.

In the operating room, a monitor alarm went off. Strange's body was flatlining. His heart had stopped. Christine ran to get defibrillator paddles.

She charged them up and shocked his heart, trying to start it again.

In the astral realm, the extra energy from the charge went off like a bomb through Stephen's projection. It blasted the lunging Zealot across the room. In the real world, equipment clanged and fell onto the floor. "Stephen, come on," Christine said. His heart started to beat...but slowly. He was still in danger.

Strange appeared to Christine. "Hit me again!"

She gave a little shriek and said, "Stop doing that!"

"Up the voltage and hit me again."

"No, your heart is beating!" On the monitor, the signal was getting stronger.

Strange knew it was against all medical protocol to shock a patient again when the first shock had worked...but in the astral realm he was still in real trouble. "Just do it!"

He vanished, just in time to avoid the Zealot, who was after him again. But this time, instead of trying to fight his way free, Strange grappled with him and held on. He heard the building whine of the defibrillator...and then Christine shocked him again.

The charge burned through Strange's astral form and into the Zealot's, overwhelming the aggressive projection. There was a violent flash, and in the real world lightbulbs popped and the operating room went dark. In the astral realm, the Zealot's body disappeared, leaving behind nothing but burned marks on the walls.

On the operating table, Strange's body spasmed and he opened his eyes. Christine jumped back, still clutching the defibrillator paddles. "Oh god! Are you okay?"

He tried to lift his head. "Hey there," he said. He was alive.

A little later, as she stitched his wound, Christine had gotten herself together enough to start getting mad. Really mad. "After all this time, you just show up here, flying out of your body?" she said, pulling a stitch tight.

"Yeah, I know," Strange said. He wished he could explain everything, but how would she take it? "I missed you, too, by the way. I wrote two e-mails, but you never responded."

She didn't look at him, keeping her attention on the sutures she was putting in his chest. She might be mad, but she was still a phenomenal doctor. "Why would I?"

"Christine, I am so, so sorry. For all of it." It felt good to say that. Whatever else happened with Kamar-Taj and Kaecilius, Strange knew he had changed as a person. "And you were right, I was a complete ass. I treated you so horribly, and you deserved so much more."

"Stop," she said. "You... you're clearly in shock."

But now she did look at him, and he saw the concern—and maybe something more—in her face. "I mean, what is happening? Where have you been?"

"Well, after Western medicine failed me, I headed East, and I ended up in Kathmandu."

"Kathmandu?" Christine rolled her eyes.

"And then I went to a place called Kamar-Taj and I talked to someone called The Ancient One and…"

"Oh," she said. "So you joined a cult."

"No, I didn't. Not exactly. I mean, they did teach me to tap into powers that I never even knew existed."

"Yeah, that sounds like a cult."

He had known it would be hard to explain, but he wasn't sure *what* he expected from Christine. "It's not a cult," he said again, thankful she wasn't outright saying he was crazy.

"Well, that's what a cultist would say." She was

right. Strange chuckled and started to sit up. "Wait, Stephen...what do you think you're doing?"

"I'm late for a cult meeting," he said, and swung his legs off the table. He could walk with some help, and Christine guided him out into the hall.

"This is insane," she said. *There it was*, he noted. He needed to be in the hospital.

"Yeah," Strange agreed. There was no point in arguing it.

"Where are you going?"

"Um..." He wasn't sure how to say it.

Christine, as usual, cut to the chase. "Just tell me the truth."

Okay, Strange thought. *You asked for it.* "Well, a powerful sorcerer, who gave himself over to an ancient entity who can bend the very laws of physics, tried very hard to kill me, but I left him chained up in Greenwich Village, and the quickest way back there is through a dimensional gateway that I opened up in the mop closet."

She let him go and took a step back. "Okay. Don't tell me. Fine."

Strange opened the closet door. The portal still hung sparking in midair, with the interior of the Greenwich Village Sanctum visible inside it. Christine walked up close enough to see that it was real, eyes wide with astonishment. Strange kept going. From the other side of the portal, he turned back to her.

"I really do have to go," he said. The portal closed as he walked away into the Sanctum.

CHAPTER 10

The body of the Zealot lay in the hall, with the cloak hovering nearby. Strange bent and laid two fingers on the Zealot's neck, feeling for a pulse.

There was none. He was dead. And Strange had killed him.

It was a terrible thing to realize, but Strange couldn't take time to process it right then. He swept the cloak around his shoulders and went upstairs looking for Kaecilius. Instead, he found the empty framework lying on the floor in the artifact gallery, under the window that displayed the Sanctum's sigil.

"Strange!" He turned and saw Mordo on the other side of the gallery, a sword strapped to his back. "You're okay."

"A relative term," Strange said. "But yeah, I'm okay."

"The Cloak of Levitation," Mordo said as he got a better look at what Strange was wearing. "It came to you."

The Ancient One stepped out of the shadows near Mordo. "No minor feat," she said, almost complimenting him. "It's a fickle thing."

Strange wasn't interested in compliments from her right then, but he also knew the time wasn't right to confront her with what he had learned about Dormammu and the source of her long life. "He's escaped," he said.

"Kaecilius?" The Ancient One asked.

"Yeah. He can fold space and matter at will."

"He folds matter outside the Mirror Dimension? In the real world?" She looked deeply concerned at this. Having experienced Kaecilius's power, Strange could understand why.

"Yeah," he said.

"How many more?"

"Two. I stranded one in the desert."

"And the other?"

"His body is in the hall," Strange said. "Master Drumm was in the foyer."

"He's been taken back to Kamar-Taj," Mordo said.

Her tone grave, The Ancient One brought Strange up to date. "The London Sanctum has fallen. Only New York and Hong Kong remain now to shield us from the Dark Dimension. You defended the New York Sanctum from attack. With its Master gone, it needs another....Master Strange."

Master? That wasn't possible. He wasn't ready;

compared to Mordo or Wong, Strange had just begun his study. And even if he was ready ... "No," he said, turning to her. "It is Doctor Strange. Not Master Strange, not Mister Strange—Doctor Strange." He struggled to control his emotions as he went on. "When I became a doctor, I swore an oath to do no harm. And I have just killed a man! I'm not doing that again. I became a doctor to save lives, not take them."

The Ancient One heard him out. From the look on her face, he even thought she believed he was sincere. But still she cut through what he said. She was her own kind of surgeon, slicing away the diseased parts of her students' minds and emotions. "You became a doctor to save one life above all others," she said. "Your own."

Strange was getting a little sick of her guru act. "Still seeing through me, are you?"

"I see what I've always seen," she said. "Your overinflated ego. You want to go back to the delusion that you can control anything, even death, which no one can control. Not even the great Doctor Stephen Strange."

"Not even Dormammu?" If she was going to come after him, Strange thought, he wasn't going to back down. Not now. "He offers immortality."

Mordo watched both of them, looking concerned that the tension between them might escalate. "It's our fear of death that gives Dormammu life," The Ancient One said. "He feeds off it."

"Like you feed on him?" Strange saw from her expression that it was true. "You talk to me about controlling death. Well, I know how you do it. I've seen the missing rituals from *The Book of Cagliostro*."

"Measure your next words very carefully, Doctor," she said, her voice quiet, hard, and distinctly threatening.

Strange didn't care. "Because you might not like them?"

"Because you may not know of what you speak."

"What is he talking about?" Mordo demanded.

He was looking at The Ancient One, but Strange answered instead. "I'm talking about her long life. The source of her immortality. She draws power from the Dark Dimension to stay alive."

Mordo refused to believe this. "That's not true."

"I've seen the rituals and worked them out," Strange said, eyes still focused on The Ancient One. "I know how you do it."

She paused, and for a moment Strange thought he might have gone too far. Where were the warnings about how far you could push the Sorcerer Supreme before she lashed out? But she stayed calm and changed the subject. "Once they regroup, the Zealots will be back. You'll need reinforcements." She turned away and was gone.

There was a long, tense silence. Then Strange broke it. "She is not who you think she is," he said to Mordo.

Mordo was loyal, and Strange's accusations against The Ancient One angered him. "You don't have the right to say that. You have no idea of the responsibility that rests upon her shoulders."

"No," Strange agreed. "And I don't want to know."

"You're a coward," Mordo said stiffly, beginning to lose his temper.

"Because I'm not a killer?"

"These Zealots will snuff us all out, and you can't muster the strength to snuff them out first?"

"What do you think I just did?" Strange shouted.

"You saved your own life!" Mordo shouted back. "And then whined about it like a wounded dog."

"When you would have done it so easily?"

"You have no idea. The things I've done...and the answer is yes. Without hesitation."

"Even if there's another way?"

"There is no other way."

"You lack imagination."

"No, Stephen," Mordo said scornfully. "You lack a spine."

Sword or no sword, Strange was ready to take a swing at Mordo, then and there...but was interrupted when they both heard the rumble and surge of a portal opening from near the Sanctum's front door. "They're back," Mordo said, and ran to the balcony overlooking the foyer.

Kaecilius and his Zealots were there, with a pulsing sphere of magical power glowing in the air nearby. "We have to end this. Now!" Mordo growled. He vaulted over the railing and dropped to the floor below.

Strange swung over the railing, too, but hung in the air, with the Cloak of Levitation holding him in place. Mordo was tangled with both Zealots while Kaecilius began performing a ritual that Strange assumed would destroy the New York Sanctum.

The Zealots had Mordo in their grasp. "Strange!" he yelled. "Get down here and fight!"

Strange was going to fight. But he had a better plan than just charging headlong into a battle. He was going to change the battlefield. He spread his arms and cast a spell he had learned from watching The Ancient One.

Kaecilius brought both arms down, just as he had inside the London Sanctum—was it only an hour ago? But instead of an explosion that destroyed the Sanctum and crippled the shield protecting Earth from the Dark Dimension, Kaecilius's blast petered out and disappeared. He looked up in surprise as Strange drifted slowly down the staircase. "The Mirror Dimension," Strange said. "You can't affect the real world in here. Who's laughing now?"

He had expected Kaecilius to be angry, or maybe even afraid. Instead, the corrupted Master looked right back at Strange with a little smile and said, "I am."

Reality began to shift around them all, matter

folding itself into new patterns. Kaecilius would turn the Sanctum into a death trap if Strange and Mordo didn't get out. Strange flew down the stairs and caught Kaecilius in the middle of casting the spell. He ripped Kaecilius's sling ring off and got out the door as Mordo fought his way free of the Zealots. Out on the Mirror Dimension version of Bleecker Street, Strange turned to Mordo. "I've got his sling ring," he said. "I mean, they can't escape, right?"

Through the folding facade of the New York Sanctum, Kaecilius and his Zealots strode out into the street. Mordo slapped him on the arm. "Run!"

They ran down Bleecker Street to Sixth Avenue, where Strange froze. The roads meeting at the intersection shifted, flipping upside down and inside out. He turned and saw streets and blocks of buildings splitting into mirror images of themselves. Cars drove by upside down above him, or appeared out of empty space to roar past him.

"Their connection to the Dark Dimension makes them more powerful in the Mirror Dimension," Mordo said. "They can't affect the real world, but they can still kill us. This wasn't clever. This was suicide!"

Kaecilius and the pair of Zealots were headed for them down the middle of the street. Strange and Mordo ran in the other direction as Strange opened a portal. If they could get out and trap Kaecilius in the Mirror Dimension, they would have time to figure out what to do next.

But before they got to their escape portal, Kaecilius tipped that entire part of New York City up on its side. Strange and Mordo skidded across the tilting street toward the skyscraper on the other side. They hit the side of a bus. Inside, an old man was laughing over a book, completely unaware of their presence.

They got to their feet and leaped up the side of the nearest tall building. Strange had the Cloak of Levitation, and Mordo the Vaulting Boots of

Valtorr. Behind them, Kaecilius was closing in...
but Strange had opened another portal on the
side of the building. They were getting close.

Kaecilius jumped into the air, and when he
landed again, the impact sent an amazing wave
of energy rolling up the building. When the
wave struck the portal, it, too, dissipated, leaving
Strange and Mordo to turn and face their enemies.
But Kaecilius wasn't done. He curved both arms
inward, and the skyscraper upon which they all
stood curled itself over toward the street. Strange
and Mordo fell off it, and as they fell, the street
below them slid apart into sections. They plum-
meted through the gap into another layer of the
folded New York Kaecilius had created, landing
on the side of another building. Around them they
saw the entire city, separated as if it were made of
puzzle pieces and Kaecilius had flung them apart.

"This *was* a mistake," Strange admitted. Mordo
gave him an incredulous look.

Then the building underneath them heaved and flung them into the air again. While they fell, the city came together and broke apart again. Mordo deflected off a fire escape and Strange lost track of him. He found himself in a maze of iron steps and railings, trying to stay ahead of the pursuing Kaecilius. The Zealots also kept pace, running on the sides and bottom of other pieces of the city as they interlocked around Strange.

In the confusion, Strange lost track of Kaecilius, too—and a moment later Dormammu's servant ran up from the bottom of the same steel catwalk Strange was following. He punched Strange hard in the gut, knocking the wind out of him. As Strange fell, Kaecilius slid his palms against each other, creating a Space Shard. Strange was down and gasping. He wouldn't be able to dodge the fatal thrust.

CHAPTER 11

A s Strange tried to get his breath back, the part of the platform where he lay separated from Kaecilius and slid away. Kaecilius's Space Shard struck sparks from the steel at his feet. Strange rolled over and started to get up. Around him, the chaotic jumble of buildings and fire escapes and streets re-formed into a circular barrier. A solid floor built itself out of parts of the city, with a powerful sigil fit into its surface.

On the other side of the enclosed space, The Ancient One stood, in a yellow robe she wore when she knew battle was at hand. She spread her fingers and the magical fans she used to fight blazed to life in both hands. As Strange got up, he saw Mordo at his side, staring in shock at The Ancient One. When he looked at her again, he understood why.

Her forehead blazed with the rune of Dormammu, just like the ones that glowed on the foreheads of Kaecilius and the two Zealots who stepped out onto the floor.

"It's true," Mordo said, his voice full of shock and hurt. "She does draw power from the Dark Dimension."

The Ancient One looked at him for a long moment, her expression betraying nothing. Then she turned her gaze on her renegade former student. "Kaecilius," she said.

They circled each other on the outer edge of the floor, with pieces of the New York cityscape swirling around them. It was like being inside a kaleidoscope. On one of the rotating pieces glowed the portal The Ancient One had used to find them in the Mirror Dimension. Strange and Mordo watched but did not intervene. This was a final reckoning between the Sorcerer Supreme and a Master who had betrayed her.

"I came to you, broken, lost, bleeding," Kaecilius said. "I trusted you to be my teacher, and you fed me lies."

"I tried to protect you," she answered.

"From the truth?"

"From yourself."

He smirked. "I have a new teacher now."

"Dormammu deceives you. You have no idea of what he truly is," she said sadly. The mark of Dormammu was gone from her forehead now. "His eternal life is not paradise, but torment."

"Liar!" Kaecilius snarled—and flanked by his Zealots, he charged.

The Ancient One moved with speed and power belying both her small frame and her great age. She dropped both Zealots as soon as they got within arm's reach and then beat back Kaecilius's charge with powerful strikes of her fans. The Zealots got to their feet again. She anticipated the first move, knocking down one Zealot again with a crackling blow of a fan and then pivoting to meet the other's lunge. He froze with The Ancient One's fan laid against the side of his throat. She could have killed him then, but she did not—and this act of mercy cost her dearly.

Kaecilius stepped up and thrust his Space Shard through the Zealot's body and into The Ancient One. She recoiled and staggered. Mordo cried out in shock. Kaecilius withdrew the Space Shard and the Zealot fell to the floor. The Ancient One was looking him in the eye when Kaecilius kicked her away. Her body flew through the air and through the portal she had created.

Strange and Mordo rushed for the portal, diving through it just as it closed. The portal deposited them high in the air over New York City. Below, The Ancient One's body was falling. She crashed through a glass awning and onto the sidewalk as pedestrians screamed and ran from the broken glass. Strange and Mordo reached the ground a moment later. Strange crouched over her body, then looked up. Once again, he knew where they could turn.

A few minutes later, they were pushing a gurney through the emergency room where Strange had just nearly died. "Christine!" he shouted.

He saw her tilt her head back and close her eyes. "Are you kidding me?" she said to no one in particular. Then she turned and saw The Ancient One on the gurney, bloodied and still. "Oh my god," she said, and ran to meet them.

"It's not fibrillation," Strange said as they headed for the operating room. "She has a stunned myocardium." That was the tissue of the heart muscle that kept the organ pumping.

She fell into stride next to the gurney. "It's neurogenic?"

"Yes." That was the closest Strange could get. He wasn't sure what the medical terminology would be for a heart stopped by a blade made of energy from the Dark Dimension.

When they got The Ancient One into surgery, they also found she had serious head injuries from the fall. Strange scrubbed in and got as far as picking up a scalpel before he realized he couldn't help.

At least . . . not as a doctor.

"Nic," he said. Nic West looked over at him, and Strange held up the scalpel. He still didn't have the steadiness to operate, and Christine had been right when she said Nic was a good surgeon. "We need to relieve the pressure on her brain."

"She's still dropping," a nurse warned. The heart monitor's alarm sounded. "We're losing her!"

"You need to increase her oxygen!" Strange said.

Christine hurried to the operating table. "I need a crash cart!"

The nurse kept calling out the patient's status. "Her pupils are dilated! No reflexes! I'm not reading any brain activity."

Strange knew what was happening. If The Ancient One's body was dying...

He projected his astral form out of his body, and naturally, there her astral form was, floating out of the room. Strange chased her. "What are you doing? You're dying!"

She didn't answer, but she did stop when she got to a wall of windows on the other side of the nurses' station. From there she could look out over the city. "You have to return to your body now," Strange urged her. "You don't have time."

"Time is relative. Your body hasn't even hit the floor yet." Strange looked out where she was looking. A helicopter hung frozen in air. Snowflakes were suspended just outside the window. Time had stopped, or at least slowed so much he couldn't see it passing. A lightning crack opened in the sky, its brilliant radiance spilling through the darkness. "I've spent so many years peering through time, looking at this exact moment. But I can't see past it. I've prevented countless terrible futures. And after each one, there's always another. And they all lead here, but never further."

"You think this is where you die," Strange said. That would be the obvious downside of being able to see the future.

"Do you wonder what I see in your future?" she asked.

"No." The Ancient One smiled at him and Strange realized that once again, she was seeing through him. "Yes."

"I never saw your future," she said, once again confounding his expectations. "Only its possibilities. You have such a capacity for goodness. You always excelled, but not because you crave success, but because of your fear of failure."

"It's what made me a great doctor." The crack in the sky disappeared. In the outside world, it was there and gone in a fraction of a second; here in the astral realm, he could track it disappearing in slow motion.

"It's precisely what kept you from greatness," she said. "Arrogance and fear still keep you from learning the simplest and most significant lesson of all."

"Which is?"

"It's not about you." She paused, waiting for him to speak. But Strange had at last learned from her when it was better to listen. "When you first came to me, you asked me how I was able to heal Jonathan Pangborn. I didn't. He channels dimensional energy directly into his own body."

"He uses magic to walk."

"Constantly. He had a choice, to return to his own life or to serve something greater than himself."

Strange remembered Pangborn saying he wasn't ready for some of what he had learned. Now he understood what that meant...and what it could mean for him. "So, I could have my hands back again? My old life?"

"You could. And the world would be all the lesser for it." *So that is the choice*, Strange thought. *My old life back, or protect Earth from Dormammu.* "I've hated drawing power from the Dark Dimension," The Ancient One went on. "But as you well know, sometimes one must break the rules in order to serve the greater good."

"Mordo won't see it that way."

"Mordo's soul is rigid and unmovable, forged by the fires of his youth. He needs your flexibility, just as you need his strength. Only together do you stand a chance of stopping Dormammu."

She was right. Strange knew it. But he was also afraid. "I'm not ready."

Another lightning bolt crept across the sky. "No one ever is," The Ancient One said. "We don't get to choose our time. Death is what gives life meaning. To know your days are numbered, your time is short. You'd think after all this time I'd be ready. But look at me, stretching one moment out into a thousand, just so I can watch the snow."

He felt her hand let his go, and when he looked over to see why, Strange was alone. The Ancient One's spirit had vanished.

She was gone. The sky was whole again.

CHAPTER 12

Back in the real world, Strange stood at the sink for a long time, letting the warm water run over his hands as he thought about The Ancient One and what he was going to do next. Christine came up next to him, and for a moment they stood there washing their hands, not needing to talk, as they had before and after countless surgeries.

Only now everything was different. Strange

hadn't operated. He couldn't. And now The Ancient One was gone, and Christine had seen things she couldn't have been ready for.

He reached out and took her hand. "Are you okay?" she asked. Strange looked over at her. He didn't know if he was okay. He didn't know if he would ever be okay again. "I don't understand what's happening," Christine said.

"I know. But I have to go right now. You said that losing my hands didn't have to be the end, that it could be a beginning."

"Yeah. Because there are other ways to save lives." She remembered.

Strange cradled her face in his hands. He had missed so much, been so wrapped up in his ego and his reputation... "A harder way."

"A weirder way," she said.

A voice over the hospital intercom interrupted them. "Doctor Palmer, the ER, please. Doctor Palmer, the ER."

"I don't want you to go," Strange said with tears in his eyes. But it was useless. She kissed him and turned away. She had obligations, after all. She had responsibilities.

So did he.

After she was gone, he took another moment at the scrub sink to get himself together. Then he put on the Cloak of Levitation again and drew its collar up. The points of the collar rubbed at the tears on his cheeks, like it was trying to clean him up. He shrugged it away. "Stop."

But at least that got his mind off Christine a bit.

Good cloak.

Kaecilius and two Zealots stepped through a portal a few blocks from the Hong Kong Sanctum. Wong knew they were coming. He had gathered the Masters and acolytes protecting the Sanctum. "Choose your weapon wisely," he said. For himself he selected the Wand of Watoomb. "No one steps foot in this Sanctum. No one."

Wong strode out of the Sanctum to meet Kaecilius. It was a warm night in Hong Kong, as most of them were. The street was crowded. Workmen putting up scaffolding, families eating at noodle shops, mopeds and cars zooming to their destinations. Kaecilius and the Zealots emerged from the crowd. Wong greeted him. "Kaecilius."

Kaecilius stopped a little distance away. "You're on the wrong side of history, Wong."

Wong dropped into a fighting stance, Wand of Watoomb at the ready. Kaecilius and the Zealots drew Space Shards out of thin air. The battle for the future of Earth was about to begin.

Strange stepped through a portal from the hospital, arriving in Kamar-Taj, and knowing he had to have a long talk with Mordo before he could confront Kaecilius once and for all. Was he ready?

He would have to be.

Mordo stood alone in the darkness, with wreckage from the earlier explosion all around him. Strange didn't have anything to say that could lighten the mood. "She's dead," he said.

"You were right," Mordo said slowly. Near him, the pedestal that once had held the Eye of Agamotto leaned on its base, almost falling over. "She wasn't who I thought she was."

"She was...complicated," Strange said. That was the best description he could find. His last conversation with her rang in his head again. The Ancient One was right. Strange needed Mordo's strength and single-minded belief in right and wrong; Mordo needed Strange's flexibility and ability to see different solutions to a problem.

"Complicated?" Mordo repeated. Strange could see he was still grieving, trying to understand how he could have been deceived for so long. "The Dark Dimension is volatile. Dangerous. What if it overtook her? She taught us it was forbidden while she drew on its power to steal centuries of life."

"She did what she thought was right." Strange believed this. As she had said, he knew the value of breaking the rules once in a while to get the needed result.

"The bill comes due," Mordo said. He sounded almost like a preacher, warning of the wages of sin. Strange wondered what had happened in Mordo's past to harden him this way. "Don't you see? Her transgressions led the Zealots to Dormammu. Kaecilius was her fault. And here we are, in the consequence of her deception. A world on fire."

"Mordo, London Sanctum has fallen. And New York has been attacked. Twice." Strange didn't have to say what they were both thinking: If they didn't do something about it, more fire was coming. The fires of the Dark Dimension—the kind that could never be put out. "You know where they're going next," Strange finished.

Of course Mordo did. "Hong Kong."

"You told me once to fight as if my life depended on it, because one day it might," Strange reminded him. He could still see Mordo dancing through the air with the Vaulting Boots of Valtorr. "Well, today is that day. I cannot defeat them alone."

Mordo looked at him quietly . . . and nodded. As Strange had known he would. He was a soldier who believed in his cause even when he no longer believed in his leaders.

Strange opened a portal to Hong Kong and they leaped through into fire and destruction.

Sirens rose and fell, echoing down the streets. Strange saw fires burning and water spouting from broken fire hydrants. People ran in every direction away from the unfolding catastrophe at the end of the block.

There, the Hong Kong Sanctum lay in ruins. And over it, the terrifying spaces of the Dark Dimension were starting to blot out the sky, swirling and crackling with the deep, unsettling colors of Dormammu's domain. "The Sanctum has already fallen," Mordo said. He looked up into the sky. "The Dark Dimension. Dormammu is coming. It's too late. Nothing can stop him."

Strange saw Kaecilius, looking pleased with himself, walking up the street toward them with his Zealots flanking him. It was a desperate time, Strange thought. The end of the world...unless he could do something about it. And maybe—just maybe—he could.

"Not necessarily," he said, and touched the middle and ring fingers of each hand together. The Eye of Agamotto opened.

"No," Kaecilius said. He sprinted toward Strange, Space Shard raised for the strike that would end the battle once and for all. . . .

Strange brought the powerful green circle into being. Bands of power encircled his arm.

Kaecilius leaped through the air. The tip of his Space Shard plunged toward Strange . . . and then slowed . . . and then stopped.

Strange held the green circle in place, making sure he had control over it. Then, slowly, he began to turn it counterclockwise.

Kaecilius flew backward through the air. Water splashed up from the pavement, and a huge aluminum and neon sign rose from the car it had crushed a minute before. Wrecked cars rolled backward and landed on the road. Strange kept it going, building on the spell until it had its own momentum. "Spell's working," he said to Mordo. "We got a second chance."

Time continued to reverse around the two of them as they ran down the street past Kaecilius and the Zealots—and toward the wreckage of the Sanctum. But Kaecilius didn't stay trapped in the spell for long. The Dark Dimension was close, yawning above Hong Kong, and its power allowed the fanatic to break free and join Strange and Mordo in their pocket of forward-moving time.

Kaecilius caught up to Strange near the Sanctum and knocked him sprawling. He was nearly hit by a car flying backward through the air. Stephen fought back, trying to get down the block as rubble flew into the air. Buildings repaired themselves, scaffoldings rose from the street. Mordo and one of the Zealots grappled in a flooded part of the street until the water suddenly rose up from the pavement in a wave, carrying her with it. A moment later, she was sealed inside an aquarium, curious fish flitting around her face.

Strange still couldn't get away from Kaecilius. The corrupted Master was there every time Strange thought he had gotten away. Mordo, having seen what happened to the Zealot, had an idea. An energy whip uncoiled from his hand and caught Kaecilius around one leg. Then Mordo flung him into the ruins of a nearby building.

"No!" Kaecilius roared, but then his voice was cut off as the building rebuilt itself around him. His body was covered in concrete and tile.

Rubble tumbled up from a pile next to a noodle stand, revealing Wong. He blinked, startled, and Strange phased him into the isolated bubble outside time. "Wong!" Then Strange realized what he was doing and remembered what Wong had said about it before. "I'm breaking the laws of nature, I know."

Wong looked around them, eyes wide open. "Well, don't stop now."

Strange looked up at the rubble of the Sanctum, slowly putting itself together into a building again. Above it, the sickly energies of the Dark Dimension receded. "When the Sanctum is restored, they will attack again. We have to defend it. Come on!"

Before they'd gone ten steps, Kaecilius had broken free of the wall holding him. He pounded a fist into the ground, creating a wave of force that slammed Strange, Wong, and Mordo to the ground.

Time slowed . . . and stopped. It didn't start going forward again, but it was no longer moving backward, either. The Sanctum hung in mid-collapse. A noodle vendor stood with a pan of noodles hanging in the air while he flipped them.

"Get up, Strange," Mordo gasped. "Get up and fight! We will finish this."

Mordo and Wong got up. Strange could barely stand.

"You can't fight the inevitable," Kaecilius said as he walked up to them. His eyes seemed to have sunk deeper into his skull, and the scaly gray decay on his face was spreading. He watched the skies, in no hurry. "Isn't it beautiful? A world beyond time. Beyond death."

"Beyond time..." Strange recalled the first time he'd looked into *The Book of Cagliostro*. Mordo had warned him of creating paradoxes, breaking the time stream...and creating loops outside of it.

He could not defeat Kaecilius face-to-face. Not with Kaecilius tapping the power of the Dark Dimension. But there was never only one solution to a problem.

The Cloak of Levitation carried Strange into the air. "Strange!" Mordo called after him. Strange wished he could explain, but there wasn't time. Soon enough, Kaecilius would break the spell holding time in place. Something had to change before then...and Strange thought he knew what to do.

"He's gone," Kaecilius said matter-of-factly as Strange disappeared into the Dark Dimension. His tone was not mocking, but definitely satisfied. "Strange has left to surrender to his power."

CHAPTER 13

Strange passed among the incredible worlds of the Dark Dimension. Some looked like giant bacteria, others burned with occult fire. They were every size, from small globes Strange could almost reach around to vast spheres that must have been larger than Jupiter or maybe even the sun. Bizarre energies crackled through the space between them. He saw nothing living, nothing that made him think anything ever had lived here. What creature could? What would want to?

Nothing. Only Dormammu. And that was who Strange had come to see.

He landed on the surface of a small world. Glowing blue vents in its surface released heat and vile gases. Strange ignored them. He spun one of the bands on his forearm, trying to lock this moment as the beginning of a loop. Had it worked? There was only one way to find out.

Near him he saw what at first looked like a violet-colored sun...but then revealed itself to be just one eye of the monstrous shape of the dread Dormammu. The ruler of the Dark Dimension was the size of a skyscraper, with a body that seemed to be made of stone and arcane fire. Strange leaped from the small globe where he'd first landed to a larger one spinning nearby, closer to Dormammu.

"Dormammu!" he shouted. "I've come to bargain."

Dormammu's face revealed itself, looming over Strange a hundred feet high. "You've come to die," he said, and his voice was like an earthquake. "Your world is now my world, like all worlds."

Shards of energy began to fall around Strange. He got his shield up and deflected them. Irritated, Dormammu roared out a stream of energy. Strange leaned into it, holding on...and then he felt the assault overwhelm his powers, and he was disintegrated in a moment.

CHAPTER 14

Dormammu!" Strange shouted. "I've come to bargain."

"You've come to die," Dormammu said, looming over Strange. "Your world is now my world.... What is this illusion?"

"No, this is real," Strange said.

"Good," Dormammu said. A moment later, Strange was impaled on stone spikes that fell from above.

CHAPTER 15

"Dormammu!" Strange shouted. "I've come to bargain."

"You…" Dormammu paused, confused. "What is happening?"

Strange took a gloating tone. The sooner he got Dormammu angry, the sooner they could get to the real bargaining. "Just as you gave Kaecilius powers from your dimension, I've brought a little power from mine." He spread his arms, with the powerful green bands of the Eye of Agamotto on each. "This is time. An endless looped time."

"You dare!" Dormammu thundered. Strange looked up and saw his fist coming down, the size of a tank and a thousand times as strong.

"Dormammu! I've come to bargain."

"You cannot do this forever," Dormammu growled.

"Actually, I can," Strange said. "This is how things are now. You and me, trapped in this moment, endlessly."

"Then you will spend eternity dying."

"Yes." Strange heard The Ancient One's words in his head. *It's not about you.* "But everyone on Earth will live."

"But you will suffer."

"Pain is an old friend," Strange said, and the violet energy blew him away again.

"Dormammu! I've come to bargain."
Stone spikes impaled him again.

"Dormammu!"
Green tentacles devoured him.

"Dormammu!"
A falling meteor crushed him.

"Dormammu!"

Slashing bolts of energy beat him to the ground...
but this time Dormammu stopped before Strange
was dead. How many times had he died? He had
lost count long ago. "You will never win," Dormammu said, his voice like giant boulders grinding
together.

"No." Strange knew Dormammu was right
about that. "But I can lose. Again and again and
again and again, forever." Strange got to his feet.
He'd never hurt so much in his life, and never been
so sure he was doing the right thing. "And that
makes you my prisoner."

"No. Stop. Make this stop! Set me free!"

Now I've got you, Strange thought. "No. I've
come to bargain."

Dormammu leaned close enough for Strange

to feel the anger radiating from him, like its own energy that could have incinerated Strange where he stood. "What do you want?"

At last, Strange thought. *We get to the point.* "Take your Zealots from the Earth," he said. "End your assault on my world. Never come back. Do it, and I'll break the loop."

et up, Strange," Mordo said. "Get up and fight! We will finish this." He dropped into a fighting stance.

Kaecilius and his Zealots walked up to them, unhurried. Kaecilius looked at the sky, churning with the energies of the Dark Dimension. "Isn't it beautiful? A world beyond time. Beyond death."

Doctor Strange slowly descended behind him. Kaecilius sensed his presence. Perhaps he sensed something else as well, but Strange would never know. "What have you done?" he said, turning to face Strange.

"I made a bargain," Strange said simply.

On Kaecilius's hands, the gray scaly decay began to spread. Tiny violet sparks flickered at its edges. "What is this?" he demanded.

"Well, it's…it's everything you ever wanted," Strange said. "Eternal life as part of the One." Then he couldn't help but crack a little smile. After all, he'd been to the Dark Dimension. Kaecilius hadn't. "You're not going to like it."

The violet energy of Dormammu's eyes crackled across Kaecilius's body and those of the Zealots. It was as if they were starting to burn, shedding parts of their physical forms as they rose into the air. They spun and tumbled up into the sky, where the Dark Dimension swallowed them. For a moment, Strange thought he saw something else moving in there. More of Dormammu's servants? He hoped he would never find out.

"I think he really should have stolen the whole book," Strange said, still looking into the Dark Dimension. "Because the warnings...the warnings come after the spells."

Wong burst out laughing. Strange couldn't believe it. All the jokes he'd made, and that line was the one Wong liked? "Oh, that's funny," Wong said after a minute.

You never could tell, Strange thought. He brought forth the green ring again, and wrenched time back into motion. First he drew it back to the point where the Sanctum was intact. Then he let it go, to run forward again. Seven billion people on Earth would live out their normal lives.

"We did it," Wong said.

Mordo nodded, but he looked solemn. "Yes. Yes, we did it. By also violating the natural laws."

"Look around you," Strange said. "It's over." Okay, maybe they had violated natural laws, but they had saved Earth from Dormammu. That seemed like a win to Strange.

"You still think there will be no consequences, Strange? No price to pay?" Mordo was hurting—Strange could see that. He was a man who had believed in The Ancient One, and now he didn't know what to believe. "We broke our rules, just like her. The bill comes due. Always. A reckoning. I will follow this path no longer." He turned his back on them and walked away, still with the sword sheathed on his back, into the chaotic swirl of Hong Kong.

Strange looked at Wong, but neither of them knew what to do. So in the end, they returned to Kamar-Taj.

The first thing Strange did was enter the innermost chamber of the library so he could replace the Eye of Agamotto. He could always come back and get it if he needed it. The chamber had been cleaned up and everything restored to its former state. It was as if Kaecilius's attack had never happened. Strange found that a little...well, strange. For a moment, he wondered.... Was it because he had manipulated time? No, of course not. It was just the dedication of the students and Masters at Kamar-Taj.

He stood at the pedestal where the Eye of Agamotto rested. At the last moment, he hesitated, unwilling to let it go. Once you had that kind of power...

The Cloak of Levitation fluttered and lifted away from him, sweeping to the far side of the room. "Okay," Strange said. He got the message. He set the Eye in its fixture.

"Wise choice," Wong commented. "You'll wear

the Eye of Agamotto once you've mastered its powers. Until then, best not to walk the streets wearing an Infinity Stone."

Infinity Stone? Was that some bit of lore that he'd missed in his reading? "A what?"

"You have a gift for the mystic arts," Wong said, "but you still have much to learn." The Eye locked into place on its pedestal and the image of the world reappeared above it. Both Wong and Strange looked at it for a long moment. "Word of The Ancient One's death will spread through the Multiverse. The Earth has no Sorcerer Supreme to defend it. We must be ready."

Billions of lives, Strange thought, still looking at the image of the turning world. He could save them all. "We'll be ready," he said.

Together they left Kamar-Taj through a portal, returning to the New York Sanctum. There was much to prepare.

EPILOGUE

Strange settled into his new role more quickly than he'd thought he would. He was learning every day, and he was good at this mystic thing. Anyone who didn't believe that could go ask Dormammu. As part of the job, he was trying to meet all the other...well, special...beings who were active on Earth, and especially in New York.

One of them was the big, blond Avenger who called himself Thor. He was sitting in the New

York Sanctum now, looking around with interest. "So, Earth has wizards now, huh?"

Strange wasn't sure how to answer such an obvious question. He also was generally uncertain about what social graces to observe with gods. He held up a teapot. "Tea?"

Thor grinned. "I don't drink tea."

"What do you drink?"

Still grinning, Thor said, "Not tea."

From out of nowhere, Strange produced a huge tankard of ale.

"So, I keep a watch list of individuals and beings from other realms that may be a threat to this world," Stephen said, getting down to business. "Your adopted brother, Loki, is one of those beings."

Thor drained the ale. All of it.

"A worthy inclusion," he said. Then, as he watched, the tankard refilled itself.

"Yeah. So, why bring him here to New York?"

"That's a long story. A family drama, that kind of thing, but . . . we're looking for my father."

"Oh, okay. So, if you've found Odin, you all will return to Asgard promptly?"

"Oh yes." Thor was grinning again. "Promptly."

"All right." Strange stood. "Let me help you."

In another part of the city, Jonathan Pangborn was working at his lathe, machining a piece of steel to a smooth, circular edge. He heard someone come into his workshop and called over his shoulder. "Can I help you?"

The stranger wore a hood. "They carried you into Kamar-Taj on a stretcher," he said softly. "Look at you now, Pangborn."

"Mordo," Pangborn said with a grin. This was

an unexpected visit. "So, what can I do for you, man?!"

"I've been away many months now and I had a revelation," Mordo said. The expression on his face started to make Pangborn nervous. "The true purpose of a sorcerer is to twist things out of their proper shape. Stealing power, perverting nature... like you."

This was serious. "I've stolen nothing," Pangborn said. "This is my power. Mine." He'd put everything he'd learned into making himself walk again. He didn't hurt anyone, he didn't tell anyone. He just wanted to get on with his life... but something told him Mordo wasn't going to let that happen. *Mordo always* had *been a bomb waiting to go off*, Pangborn thought. He was a black-and-white kind of guy. Either your best friend or your worst enemy. And it looked like he'd decided Pangborn was on the wrong side.

Mordo saw Pangborn reaching for the crowbar

resting on his work shelf. He dodged Pangborn's swing with no trouble and thrust an open hand into Pangborn's belly. Pangborn cried out as Mordo drew the glowing essence of Pangborn's power out.

Pangborn fell to the ground, unable to move his legs again. "Power has a purpose," Mordo said. He closed his fist and Pangborn's power disappeared.

"Why are you doing this?" Pangborn groaned.

Mordo knelt in front of him, pleased with what he had done. "Because I see at long last what is wrong with the world," he said.

"Too many sorcerers."

It was an argument he planned to have with Stephen Strange....

Soon.

TURN THE PAGE FOR AN EXCERPT FROM

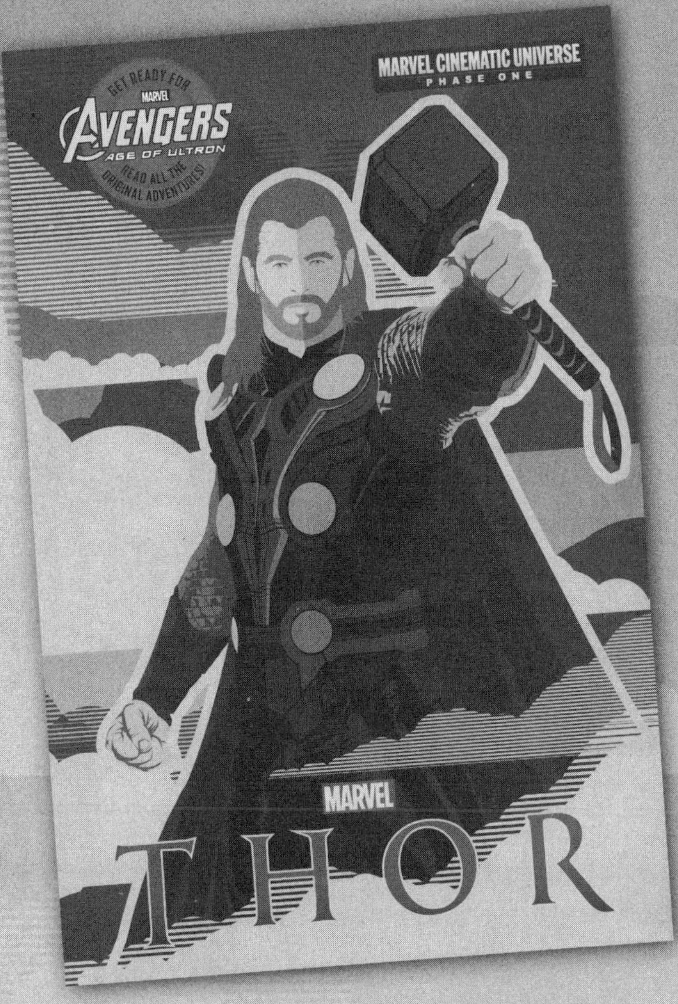

AVAILABLE NOW!

Inside the throne room, Asgardians had gathered to bid farewell to their current king and welcome their new one. Ceremonial banners fluttered from the high ceilings while attendants handed out golden goblets full of sweet drinks to the beautifully dressed guests. There was a festive air to the room as people chatted softly to each other and waited with eager anticipation for the arrival of the royal family.

At the front of the room, Thor's best friends and fellow warriors, Volstagg, Fandral, Hogun, and Lady Sif, stood at attention while members of the palace guard lined up in formation. Then Frigga entered the room and walked down the long aisle, Loki by her side. Her hair cascaded over her shoulders and down her back in ringlets that matched her golden gown. When they had made their way to the front of the room, another horn sounded, and the guards stepped aside. There was an audible gasp.

Odin sat atop his golden throne. On his head he wore a large helmet, and in his hand he gripped the mighty spear Gungnir.

Looking out over the room, Odin sighed deeply. Even after ruling for tens of thousands of years, he felt as if it were only a day ago that his father had crowned him in a ceremony similar to this one. He wondered now if his father had had the same doubts about him that he was having about Thor. *Did he regret having to step aside for the younger generation to take over?* Odin thought. *Was I as impulsive then as Thor is now? Does that mean that he, too, will grow into a wise king in time?*

Odin's thoughts were interrupted by another gasp from the crowd. Then the room erupted in applause. The mighty Thor had arrived.

Thor raised Mjolnir, the hammer that only the

worthy could lift, high over his head and soaked in the adoration. His body was covered in battle armor with large metal disks on the front chest plate. His winged helmet sat on his head, and his long red cape flowed behind him. While moments ago, everyone had believed Odin to be the most powerful ruler they would ever have, the appearance of Thor made them believe otherwise. Standing there, he looked every inch a king.

When the cheering faded, Thor finally strode up the long aisle, a smug smile on his face. Clearly the concerns of his father did not trouble Thor. He felt more than ready to rule Asgard. He had watched his father do it for years, and he thought it was time for a fresh start. He had proven himself to be one of the finest warriors the realm had ever seen. Now he would prove himself to be one of its finest kings.

As Odin watched his son walk toward him, the gravity of the situation hit the All-Father hard.

Though sometimes brash and irresponsible, Thor had grown into a fine young man. And now he was about to take the throne as the new ruler of Asgard. Odin could still vividly remember when Thor was just a boy, learning how to hold a sword for the first time. Or when he was first able to wield Mjolnir. How the hammer, which now looked small in his large hands, had nearly toppled Thor!

Odin smiled now, thinking back on that day. Learning to be king would be like learning to ride a horse. Thor wouldn't like having to go slowly, and he would fall a few times, but his difficulties would serve to teach him some valuable lessons. Or so Odin hoped. He could be only grateful that the realm was at peace and had been for a long time. There was no doubt Thor was a good warrior—but a warrior king? That was another story. That was something he had yet to learn.

Finally, Thor arrived in front of his father. He nodded at his mother and brother and friends and then knelt, bowed his head, and waited. A hush fell over the crowd as they, too, waited.

"A new day has come for a new king to wield his own weapon," Odin began, his deep voice echoing through the room. "Today, I entrust you with the sacred throne of Asgard. Responsibility, duty, honor. They are essential to every soldier and every king." As the All-Father spoke, Thor raised his eyes to look at him. Odin willed the words to impact his son, to get through to him. For after this day, he would be on his own.

Odin continued, repeating the declaration that had been spoken to him so many years before. He was at the very end of his speech when he felt it—a chill that cut through the room and caused people to shiver uncertainly. Odin's heart began to race. He had felt this chill before—on Jotunheim. Asgard had waged a long and fierce war with the ice realm. But a truce had been made years ago.

There was no reason for Odin to think Jotuns would be in Asgard. Still...

Shaking off the feeling of dread, Odin continued. He was just about to say the final words that would make Thor king when the banners hanging from the ceiling suddenly iced over.

There was no denying it. "Frost Giants," Odin whispered.